She bit her lip. "So I decided I should come here and have an affair with you and perhaps I'd get pregnant—I'm sorry...."

Cal's eyes narrowed. "What made you confess?"

"I couldn't use you like that," Joanna said in a low voice. "Or deceive you. It would be wrong."

She sat up, wishing Cal would pull the sheets over the sculpted lines of his torso. Confession or no, she still wanted him. Her whole body was an ache of unfulfilled desire.

He said in a peculiar voice, "You know, this could all work out for the best. You could have a baby, my daughter could have a mother and as for me—why, I could wake up every morning to find you in my bed."

A cold fist clamped around Joanna's heart. "What are you talking about?"

"Marriage," he said.

"Marriage?" she squawked.

Back by popular demand…

EXPECTING!

She's sexy,
successful…
and
PREGNANT!

Relax and enjoy our fabulous series
about couples whose passion ends in
pregnancies…sometimes unexpected! Of course,
the birth of a baby is always a joyful event, and
we can guarantee that our characters will
become wonderful moms and dads—but what
happened in those nine months before?

Share the surprises, emotions, drama and
suspense as our parents-to-be come to terms
with the prospect of bringing a new baby
into the world. All will discover that the
business of making babies brings with it
the most special love of all….

Delivered only by Harlequin Presents…

Sandra Field

PREGNANCY OF CONVENIENCE

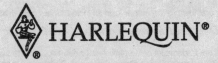

TORONTO • NEW YORK • LONDON
AMSTERDAM • PARIS • SYDNEY • HAMBURG
STOCKHOLM • ATHENS • TOKYO • MILAN • MADRID
PRAGUE • WARSAW • BUDAPEST • AUCKLAND

ISBN 0-373-12329-9

PREGNANCY OF CONVENIENCE

First North American Publication 2003.

CHAPTER ONE

CAL FREEMAN turned the wipers on high and slid the clutch of his four-wheel-drive into a lower gear. Not that it helped. The snow blowing horizontally across the windshield enveloped him in a world of white, through which he could, occasionally, sight the tall poles that marked the edges of this narrow road across the prairie.

The visibility had been better on the northeast ridge of Everest, he thought semi-humorously. Although the cold was almost comparable. He would never have expected conditions like this in southern Manitoba, not even in January. His friend Stephen had been right to insist that Cal carry emergency supplies when he set off to visit the Strassens, whose isolated home was several miles from the nearest village.

That climb on Everest had been—literally—one of the high points of Cal's life. The struggle through the pinnacles, the bitter north winds, their decision to shoot for the top without oxygen...suddenly Cal snapped back to the present, his foot hitting the brake. What was that in the ditch to his left? A vehicle?

The snow whirled across the road like a phalanx of ghosts; he could see nothing but a smothering whiteness that mocked his normally acute vision. Slowing to a crawl, Cal peered through the glass. Perhaps it had been his imagination. After all, he and Stephen had stayed up late last night, catching up on the four-year gap since they'd last seen each other. And he'd drunk more than his fair share of that excellent Bordeaux.

No. There it was again, an angular shape skewed sideways into the ditch, hood tight against a telephone pole. Coming to a halt as close to the side of the road as he dared, Cal switched on his signal lights: not that he really expected to meet anyone else mad enough to be out in such weather. Then he hauled the hood of his down parka over his head and yanked on his gloves.

He wouldn't find anyone in the vehicle. Not in this bitter cold. But it was just as well to check.

As he stepped from the heated comfort of his Cherokee onto the road, the blizzard struck him with vicious force. The wind chill, he knew from the radio, was in the danger zone: frostbite on exposed skin within a couple of minutes. Well, he was used to that. He tucked his chin into his chest, fighting his way across the icy ruts in the dirt track, limping a little from an old knee injury. How ironic it would be if he, a world-renowned mountaineer, were to slip and break an ankle in one of the flattest places on the planet.

An irony he could do without.

The vehicle was a small white car. Bad choice, he thought trenchantly. And damn lucky the car hadn't slid completely into the ditch, in which case neither he nor anyone else would have seen it.

There was a brief lull in the wind. His heart skipped a beat. Someone was slumped over the wheel. A man or a woman? He couldn't tell.

Forgetting his knee, he lunged forward, adrenaline thrumming through his veins. The engine wasn't running; how long since the car had gone off the road? He scrubbed at the window with his gloved fist, and saw that the driver was a woman. Hatless, he thought grimly. Didn't she know better? Also, unless he was mistaken, unconscious. He grabbed the door handle, and discovered that it was locked. So were all the other doors. He pounded on the glass, yelling as loudly as he could, but the figure draped over the wheel didn't even stir.

Cal raced back to his vehicle and grabbed the shovel from the back seat. Then he staggered across the road again. Once again he banged on the window, but to no effect. Grimacing, he raised the handle of the shovel and hit the glass in the back window with all his strength. On the third try it shattered.

Quickly he unlocked the driver's door and pulled it open. Taking the woman by the waist, he lifted her awkwardly, trying to pillow her face in his shoulder. Once again he made the trip across the ice and drifts back to his vehicle. He eased her into the passenger seat, supporting her as best he could as he anchored her in place with the seat belt. Then he hurried back to her car, picked up her briefcase and threw it on the back seat of his four-wheel-drive. Clambering in on the driver's side, he turned the fan up to its highest setting, dragged off his parka and draped it over the woman's body, then tucked the synthetic silver emergency blanket around her legs. Only then did he really take a look at her.

The blizzard, the cold, the loud whir of the fan all dropped away as though they didn't exist. Cal's heart leaped in his chest. He'd never seen a woman so beautiful. So utterly and heartbreakingly beautiful. Her skin smooth as silk, her hair with the blue-black sheen of a raven's wing, her features perfect, from the softly curved mouth to the high cheekbones and exquisitely arched brows.

He wanted her. Instantly and unequivocally.

Cal swallowed hard, fighting his way back to sanity. Sanity and practicality. There was a bruised swelling on her forehead, where presumably she'd struck the windshield when the car had swerved into the light pole. Her face was as white as the whirling snow crystals, her skin cold to the touch, her breathing shallow. The most beautiful woman he'd ever seen? Was he crazy?

She was lucky to be alive. Besides, he didn't believe in love at first sight. A ludicrous concept.

So why was the hand he'd touched to her cheek burning as though it were on fire?

With an impatient exclamation, he checked the odometer. Less than three miles to the Strassens'. His best bet was to take her straight there. The sooner she was in a warm house and regained consciousness, the better. Unless he was mistaken—and he'd picked up a fair bit of medical expertise over the years—she was just concussed. Concussed and very cold.

He eased into first gear and out into the middle of the road, forcing himself to focus on staying between the ditches. He'd expected to arrive at the Strassens long before this; he hoped they weren't worried about him. His errand, after all, wasn't the most pleasant.

Dusk was falling, making the visibility even poorer. Snatching occasional glances at his passenger, whose head was now lolling on her chest, Cal shifted into third gear. A lot of the snow was being whipped from the fields, for there was nothing to stop the wind but the occasional line of trees along a creek. He'd always had plenty of respect for heights; he'd have more for flatness from now on, he decided with a wry twist of his mouth that simultaneously acknowledged he was concentrating on the weather so he wouldn't have to think about the woman.

She was probably married to a local farmer and had a clutch of raven-haired children. Why hadn't he checked to see if she was wearing a wedding ring?

What did it matter whether she was or she wasn't? The Strassens would know her name, they'd make the necessary phone calls, and she'd vanish from his life as precipitately as she'd entered it.

He'd seen lots of beautiful women in his life. Been married to one for nine years. So why had the startling purity of a stranger's profile, the elegance of her bone structure, affected him as though he were nearer his thirteen-year-old daughter's age than his own age of thirty-six?

Swearing under his breath as the gale flung snow across his path, Cal strained to see the poles along the road. He'd covered nine and a half miles since he'd left the main highway; if the Strassens' directions were right, he had another half a mile to go. Not for the first time, he found himself wondering about them, this elderly couple whose only son Gustave, a fellow mountaineer, had met his death on Annapurna just three months ago.

He, Cal, had come all this way to bring them their son's climbing gear and the few personal effects Gustave had had with him on his last expedition. An errand of mercy he'd be glad to have over and done with. His original plan had been to stay a decent length of time and then head back to the city tonight. But the weather was putting paid to that; he'd probably have to stay overnight. Not what he would have chosen, particularly as he'd never met Gustave Strassen.

An illusory gleam of lights caught his eye through the snow. That must be the Strassens' house. Now all he had to do was navigate the driveway.

Four minutes later, he was parked as near to the front door as possible. The house wasn't as substantial as he'd somehow expected. Leaving the engine running, he took the front steps two at a time and rang the doorbell.

The door opened immediately. A heavy-set man with a grizzled beard boomed, "Come in, come in out of the cold, you must be Mr. Freeman—what, no jacket?"

"Cal Freeman," Cal said rapidly. "Mr. Strassen, I have a passenger, a woman whose car went off the road. She struck her head, she needs attention right away—can I bring her in?"

The older man took a step backward. "A woman? What do you mean, a woman?"

What kind of question was that? "A young woman. On her own," Cal said impatiently, "and obviously unprepared for the weather. She ended up in the ditch. I'll go get her."

"But we—"

Cal, however, had already turned back to his vehicle, the snow stinging his cheeks. Trying to keep the woman covered as best he could, he lifted her from the seat and with his knee shoved the door shut. The wind seized the hood of his parka and flung it away from her face. For a moment that was out of time he saw her lashes flicker—long dark lashes like smudges of soot. Her lips moved, as though she were trying to speak. "It's okay," he said urgently, "you're safe now, you don't have to worry." Then he headed up the steps again.

Dieter Strassen held the door open. But he was no longer smiling. He said, his accent very pronounced, "That woman is not welcome in my house."

Cal stopped dead, leaning back against the door to close it. "*What* did you say?"

A strained voice spoke from behind Dieter. "Get her out of here! I never want to see her again. Never, do you hear me?"

Cal knew instantly that this must be Maria Strassen, Dieter's wife and Gustave's mother. Short, thin as a rail, her hair in a gray-threaded bun skewered with pins. With a gesture that might have been funny had it not been so venomous, she thrust out one hand, palm toward Cal, as though she were about to push him physically back out into the blizzard.

Him and his burden.

"Look," Cal said, "I don't know what's going on here, but this woman needs help. She's concussed and she's cold.

She needs some hot food and a warm bed. Surely you can provide those?''

With a depth of bitterness that shocked Cal, Dieter said, ''Better had she died.''

''Like our son,'' Maria flashed. ''Our beloved Gustave.''

Cal said flatly, ''How far is it to the next house?''

''Four miles,'' Dieter said.

''Surely you can see that I can't go that far,'' Cal said forcefully, shifting the weight in his arms. ''Not in this storm. I don't know who this woman is or what she's done to make you hate her, but—''

''If we hate her, Mr. Freeman, it is for very good reasons,'' Dieter said with something approaching dignity. ''You must allow us to be the judge of that.''

''She married our Gustave,'' Maria said icily. ''Married him and destroyed him.''

Cal gaped at her, the pieces belatedly falling into place. As though he had actually been picked up and moved, he found himself back in an alpine campsite overlooking the south side of Mont Blanc. Four weeks ago.

It was unseasonably warm for December, and Cal was in his bare feet, luxuriating in the damp grass beneath his toes after an arduous day hiking; he'd been testing some footwear for a friend who designed alpine boots. One of the guides who had just brought up a party of Germans and who had introduced himself to Cal as Franz Staebel, remarked, ''Gustave always liked to be in his bare feet after a climb...did you ever meet Gustave Strassen?''

''Oddly enough, no,'' Cal answered. ''Our paths nearly crossed several times but we never actually met...I was very sorry to hear about his death.''

''Ah, yes,'' Franz said, grimacing into the sun. ''He was an excellent climber, one of the best. Such a waste.'' With sudden ferocity he banged an ice pick into the ground. "A totally unnecessary waste."

"Oh?" said Cal, leaning back against the scaly trunk of a rowan tree. "How so?"

"His wife," Franz said, pulling the pick out with a strong twist of his wrist. "His wife, Joanna. She was pregnant, he'd just found out the day before. But there was a good chance the baby wasn't his. She'd cheated on him, had for years."

"Why did he stay with her, then?" Cal asked idly.

"You should have seen her. Beautiful in a way few women are. And her body...Gustave was only human." Moodily Franz kicked at a clump of grass he'd dislodged, the pale sun gleaming in his red hair. "So Joanna and the baby were on his mind that morning, the morning he attempted the rock ridge on Annapurna 3. And died in the attempt."

As Cal knew all too well, distractions could be fatal on the mountains, where a moment's misjudgment could send a man to his death. "I'm sorry," he said inadequately. "I hadn't heard about his wife before."

"She controlled the purse strings, too. A rich woman, who let Dieter be stuck with second-rate equipment, and forced him to beg for sponsorships for his climbs. Ah, it was bad. Very bad. How that man suffered."

"Where was he from?"

"Central Canada." Franz gave a bark of laughter. "The prairies. Not a hill in sight. His parents live there still."

"I have a good friend in Winnipeg," Cal remarked. "I've known him for years."

Franz sat up straight, dropping the pick on the grass. "You do? Would you be interested in visiting your friend and also doing a last favor for a climber who deserved better than the fate he met?"

"What do you mean?"

"I have Gustave's gear back in Zermatt. I was going to mail it to his parents. But how much better if it could be delivered to them personally by a fellow mountaineer."

Cal said slowly, "I do have a week or so free early in the new year...after I bring my daughter back to school here in Switzerland. And it would be great to see Stephen and his wife again. Providing they're around."

"It would help the Strassens a great deal. Their hearts must be broken. Gustave's wife, she wasted no time after his death—she got rid of the baby. It could have been Gustave's child, that was certainly possible...in which case she got rid of the Strassens' grandchild, their only connection to their dead son." He spat on the grass. "I curse the day Gustave married that woman. She brought him nothing but grief."

"Mr. Freeman?" Dieter Strassen said, with the air of a man repeating himself.

With a visible start, Cal came back to the present; and to the simple and horribly unwelcome fact that the woman in his arms was the direct cause of a good man's death and the deep grief of that man's parents. "Sorry," he mumbled, and tried to pull himself together. There was no reason in the world for him to feel so massively disillusioned about a woman he hadn't even known existed half an hour ago. An unconscious woman, to boot, with whom he hadn't exchanged as much as a word.

"Mr. Strassen," he said, "I can see my arrival here is causing you and your wife great distress, and I apologize for that. But right now I don't see any way around it. I can't just dump her in the snow, no matter what she's done."

"So you know the story?" Dieter said sharply.

"Franz Staebel, the alpine guide who had your son's

gear, told me about your daughter-in-law a month or so ago.''

"Gustave thought highly of Franz.'' Moving like a much older man, Dieter turned to his wife. "Maria, we'll put her in the back bedroom, it's the only thing we can do. She'll be gone by morning.''

"Someone else can look after her,'' Maria said in a stony voice.

Into the silence Cal said, "I will.''

"That would be best,'' Dieter said with evident relief. "I'll show you the room, and in the meantime Maria will heat some soup for you. We are being bad hosts, Mr. Freeman.'' He gave a rather rusty bow. "Welcome to our home.''

Two could play that game. "Thank you,'' Cal said, and smiled at Maria.

Her response was as cold as a glacier. "That woman will leave here tomorrow morning,'' she said, "and she must never come back.''

Cal's brain, which seemed to have gone to mush since finding a raven-haired beauty on the side of the road, finally made the connection. "Oh, of course—she'd just been here?''

"She had the audacity to bring us Gustave's silver watch, his album of family photos. As though that would make us take her in. Forgive her for all that she's done.''

"Now, Maria,'' Dieter warned.

"Our grandchild,'' Maria quavered, "she even destroyed our grandchild. Aborted it.''

"According to Gustave, it might not have been his child,'' Dieter said wearily, running his fingers through his thatch of grizzled hair. "Gustave radioed a message out the very day he died, Mr. Freeman. About the pregnancy and his doubts. He wanted to divorce her.'' His gaze flicked contemptuously over the woman in Cal's arms. "But he knew that would mean no contact with a child who could be of our own flesh and blood.''

Maria bit off her words. "She took everything from us.''

"Enough, now,'' her husband said. "I'm sure once Mr. Freeman has settled her, he'll be hungry.''

"Please call me Cal...and some soup would be delicious,'' Cal said with another smile.

Maria turned on her heel in the direction of the kitchen. Dieter lead the way along a narrow hallway to a back annex of the house; the furnishings were sparse, Cal noticed, glancing into what appeared to be a formal parlor, everything immaculately tidy and painfully clean. The back bedroom was no exception. It was also very cold.

Dieter said, "You must excuse my wife, Mr.—Cal. She is very bitter, understandably so. I'll leave you to settle in, and whenever you're ready, please come through to the dining room.''

Cal laid Joanna Strassen on the double bed, straightened, and said forthrightly, "Once she comes to, she'll need something hot to eat.'' And with annoyance realized he'd adopted the Strassens' habit of referring to Joanna Strassen as *she*. Never by name.

"I'll look after that. And I'll show you to your bedroom in the main house.''

"I think I'd better stay here and keep an eye on your daughter-in-law,'' Cal said with a depth of reluctance that took him by surprise. But if he didn't look after her, who would? "After a blow on the head, it's always a good idea to be under supervision for at least twelve hours.''

"Whatever you say,'' Dieter replied, and for a moment directed a look of such implacable hostility toward the unconscious woman on the bed that, even knowing the story, Cal was chilled to the bone. "There's extra bedding in the cupboard and the couch makes another bed,'' Dieter went on, just as though nothing had happened. "I'll see you in a few minutes."

As soon as the door closed behind him, Cal went into action. He drew the curtains against the snow that lashed the windowpanes, jammed the thermostat up several notches, and swiftly built a fire in the woodstove that stood in the corner. Touching a match to it, he watched briefly as the flames gained hold. Then he turned to the woman on the bed.

Joanna Strassen. Widow of Gustave. By all accounts an unfaithful and ungenerous wife, who apparently had destroyed her own child.

Nothing he'd learned made her any less beautiful.

CHAPTER TWO

CAL rubbed his palms down the sides of his cords, and with the same deep reluctance that he'd felt a few moments ago, approached the bed. Resting his palm on Joanna's cheek, trying to ignore the satin smoothness of her skin, he registered how cool she felt. He pulled off her gloves, chafing her cold fingers between his warmer ones. Ringless fingers, he noticed. Long and tapered, with neatly kept nails. She wore no jewelry, which rather surprised him. He met a lot of women, one way or another, and because he was rich and unmarried, spent a fair bit of energy keeping them at bay; most of them dripped with diamonds. So why didn't the wealthy widow, Joanna Strassen?

As though he had spoken her name out loud, she moved her head restlessly on the pillow, her lashes flickering. Her left hand plucked at his parka, trying to pull it around her chin. Then she gave a tiny moan of pain, a deep shudder rippling the length of her body.

Quelling an instinctive surge of compassion, Cal eased off her boots, practical low-heeled boots that looked as though they came from a factory outlet. Definitely not leather. This, like her lack of rings, seemed oddly out of character. Her tights were black, her plain sweater a deep blue. Her figure was just as much an attention-grabber as her face, he thought grimly, and almost with relief noticed that she was shivering. Hastily he pulled the covers from underneath her body, then tucked them around her.

The room was noticeably warmer, so much so that Cal stripped off his own thick wool sweater. Catching a glimpse of himself in the mirror by the door, he ran his fingers through his disordered hair, which was the dark brown of

17

polished leather. As for the rest, he'd always figured he had the right number of features in the right places and that was that. He'd never understood his appeal to women, blind to the unrevealing gray of his eyes, the strength of his chin and jaw, the flat planes of his cheeks and his air of self-containment, which many might see as a challenge. He'd been rather less than amused just before Christmas, when he was trying to avoid the attentions of a local divorcée, to have his daughter Lenny say to him impatiently, "You don't understand why every woman you meet is after you? Get a grip, Dad. You're a hunk. Big-time macho man. You should hear the girls in my school go on about you."

"Oh no, I shouldn't."

Lenny had rolled her eyes. "You're also intelligent, rich, charming when you want to be, rich, and a famous mountaineer. Oh, and did I mention rich? I rest my case."

"Rich you got right," he'd replied. "The rest—forget it."

Lenny had laughed and cajoled him into helping her with some supplemental geometry, a subject that was as much a mystery to her as literature was a delight. Cal loved his daughter Lenny more than he could imagine loving anyone else in the world...more than he'd loved her mother for the last few years of his marriage, he could now admit that to himself. Although never to Lenny.

He should remarry. Settle down and provide a proper home for Lenny, add a woman's presence to her life. Trouble is, he didn't want to. Nor had he met anyone who gave him the slightest desire to embrace—for the second time—the state of holy matrimony.

If only he didn't travel so much; it made it more difficult with Lenny. He'd curtailed his mountain-climbing expeditions the past few years. But he also had to travel for his work. Cal had inherited money from his adventurous, immigrant father; after multiplying this money many times over in a series of shrewd investments, he'd purchased an international brokerage firm; then, later, a chain of prestigious auction houses in Europe and New York, dealing with antiques and fine art. Although computer technology had cut back a certain amount of travel, there was still no substitute for a hands-on approach to his various business concerns.

One more reason why Lenny was in a private school in Switzerland.

The woman on the bed gave another of those low moans. Cal came back to the present, thrusting a birch log into the heart of the flames, and turning his attention to the bed. Despite the heaped-up bedclothes and the warmth of the room, Joanna Strassen was still shivering. Moving very slowly, his eyes trained on her face, Cal lifted the covers and got into bed beside her. Gathering her in his arms, he drew the whole length of her body toward his.

She fit his embrace perfectly, as though she had been made for it. Her cheek was resting against his bare throat, her breath softly wafting his skin; he could feel her tremors, the small rise and fall of her breathing against his chest, and the firm swell of her breasts pressed to his rib cage.

His body's response was unmistakable. He still wanted her. No matter what she'd done.

Gritting his teeth, Cal thought about the ice ridges of Brammah, the ice cliffs of Shivling, the glaciers of Everest. All to no avail. Cursing himself inwardly, he then tried to imagine she was a fellow climber with hypothermia and that he was simply doing the medically correct thing.

Equally useless. Her skin was sweetly scented, her hair in its thick braid gleamed in the firelight as though the flames themselves were caught there, and each shiver that rippled through her slender frame he felt as though it were his own body. He'd been too long without a woman, that was his problem. After all, how long had it been?

If he had to struggle to remember, it had been altogether too long. Time he rectified that. Soon. And when better than now, with Lenny in school in faraway Switzerland?

There was that blonde in Manhattan, he'd met her at a

charity ball; she'd insisted he take her phone number, he must have it somewhere. She'd certainly given every signal that she was willing to climb into his bed, no questions asked.

He couldn't even remember her name. Shows what kind of an impression she'd made.

There was also Alesha in Paris, Jasmine in Boston, Rosemary in London and Helga in Zurich. All of whom he'd dated; none of whom he'd slept with.

Joanna Strassen stirred in his arms. Hastily Cal eased his hips away from hers, wondering if her shivering had lessened slightly. The sooner he got out of this particular bed, the better.

The woman in Manhattan had had a diamond pin stuck through her left nostril. That he did remember. No wonder he hadn't phoned her.

A shudder suddenly ripped through Joanna's body. Her eyes flew open, wide with terror, and with a strength that shocked Cal she pushed hard against his chest. "No!" she cried. "No, I won't—" Then, with another of those racking shudders, she stared full at him. He saw her swallow, watched with a flash of admiration as she fought to subdue the terror that only a moment ago had overwhelmed her.

The terror that Gustave had come back from the grave to haunt her? His admiration vanished. But before he could speak, she muttered, "You're not Gustave…oh God, I thought you were Gustave." Her voice rose in panic. "Who are you? Where am I?"

"No," Cal said evenly, "I'm not Gustave. Gustave's dead, remember?"

Again terror flooded her eyes, eyes that were the sapphire blue of her sweater. As she pushed away from him, jerking her head back, she gave a sudden sharp cry of pain. Bringing one hand to her forehead, she faltered, "Please…where am I? I—I don't understand…"

No wonder Gustave Strassen had returned again and again to his faithless wife. If he, Cal, had thought her beautiful when she was unconscious, how much more so was she with emotions crossing her face, with her eyes huge and achingly vulnerable in the firelight? He said with a deliberate brutality that at some level he was ashamed of, "You had an accident. You're at Dieter and Maria Strassens' house."

Her body went rigid with shock. Then she brought both hands to her face, briefly closing her eyes. "No," she whispered, "no...tell me that isn't true."

"It's true. Where else was I to bring you? They, I might add, were no happier taking you in than you are to find yourself here."

"They hate me," she whispered, and for a moment the blue of her irises shimmered with unshed tears. "I don't want to be here! Ever again."

Either she was an accomplished actress, shedding a few tears to brilliant effect; or else everything he'd been told about her actions and character was inaccurate. Gustave, Franz, Deiter and Maria; were all of them wrong? It didn't seem very likely. Cal said coolly, "Little wonder they hate you."

She edged even further from him in the bed, her wince of pain instantly disguised. "Who are you?"

"Fate?" he said, raising one brow.

"Stop playing with me," she pleaded, and again tears glimmered on her lashes. "Please...I don't understand what's going on, you've got to tell me."

"I'm the guy who happened along the road after you'd run smack-dab into a telephone pole. You should be thanking me. With the car not running, you'd have frozen to death in short order."

"The car..." She frowned. "I remember now, I got into the car and left here. It was snowing and windy, but the roads are so straight, I was sure I'd be all right."

"It wasn't exactly the most intelligent course of action," Cal said bluntly.

"I couldn't bear to stay! And they wanted me gone, they

almost pushed me out the door. But once I was out on the road, I couldn't see where I was going and then suddenly that pole was right in front of me…the last thing I remember was turning off the ignition because I was afraid of fire.''

"One more dumb move to add to the rest.''

"So they told you about me,'' she said quietly. "And you believe them.''

"Is there any reason why I shouldn't?'' Cal demanded; and discovered to his inner consternation that he did indeed want to be supplied with those reasons.

"Oh God…'' she whispered.

She looked utterly forlorn. In one swift movement Cal rolled out of bed. "I'll go and get you some soup now that you're awake. Then I'll run a hot bath for you.''

She tried to sit up, but a wave of dizziness forced her back to the pillow. "Just go away,'' she quavered. "Go away and leave me alone.''

If only that were possible. "You don't like being confronted with the consequences of your actions, do you?'' Cal said. "I suppose I should be congratulating you on having the rudiments of a conscience.''

"Stop! Just stop—I can't take any more.''

She did indeed look at the end of her tether. Cal bit his lip, feeling uncomfortably like the school bully that had made his life a misery when he was seven and small for his age. Now that he was six-foot-two and entirely capable of looking after himself, he made it a practice never to throw his weight around. Especially with a woman. On the other hand, he was damned if he was going to apologize. When all was said and done, nothing could bring Gustave back to life. And wasn't that the bottom line?

He said coldly, "I'll be back in a few minutes. The bathroom's through that door and if I were you, I'd stay in this part of the house. You're not welcome elsewhere.''

"You think I don't know that?'' she retorted with a flash of spirit.

"Yet you're the one who came here. Uninvited, I'm sure."

"If you think I'm going to justify myself to you, you're mistaken," she said bitterly, turning her face away from him.

The flickering gold light illuminated the exquisite curve of her cheekbone. Dragging his gaze away, Cal strode out of the room. In the hallway he stood still for a minute, trying to subdue the turmoil of emotion in his chest. What was the matter with him? Yelling at a woman with a concussion? Thoroughly disliking her and wanting to kiss her senseless all in the same breath?

Disliking her was fine. She was, after all, a liar and a cheat, according to people who'd known her intimately. But kiss her? Was he out of his mind?

Lots of women had deep blue eyes and long black hair. Grow up, Cal. Or, as Lenny would say, get a grip.

After checking with Dieter he made a couple of phone calls, to Stephen with his change of plans, and to the airport, where he discovered all flights were canceled. Maria had set a place for him at the plain oak table in the dining room. Mechanically he ate a bowl of delicious wild mushroom soup and some homemade rolls, along with a salad of fresh greens, making conversation with her and her husband as best he could.

At the end of the meal Cal said, "Gustave's things are in the back of my vehicle—would you like me to bring them in now, or tomorrow morning?"

"Tomorrow would be better," Dieter said heavily. "Today, already we have been through enough."

Maria said frostily, "I have put some soup on a tray. You will take it to her."

"Of course," Cal said. "That was delicious, Maria, thank you."

"We start our day early," Dieter added. "Living as we do so isolated, we keep to a strict routine. Breakfast at eight?"

"Thanks, that would be fine," Cal said, picking up the tray Maria had deposited on the table. "I'll see you then."

He walked back along the hallway, again glancing into the parlor. The only books were thick, leather-bound tomes, the photos on the wall were of grim-faced ancestors, and there wasn't an ornament in sight. Had the house always been this joyless? This austere? Had Gustave grown up in these stark surroundings, or were they a product of Dieter and Maria's middle age?

Either way, Gustave Strassen was beginning to have his entire sympathy.

When Cal went back into the bedroom, his socked feet soundless on the bare hardwood, Joanna Strassen was lying flat on her back, gazing up at the ceiling. Her brow was furrowed, as though she were in pain; the white pillowslips and her cheeks were exactly the same color. A floorboard creaked beneath his heel. She gave a visible start, just as quickly controlled; the face she turned to him was empty of expression.

He said, "I'll help you sit up."

"I can manage."

"Don't be so dammed stubborn!"

Defiance flared in her eyes. But with that same super-human control, she subdued it. Where had she learned such control? And why?

And why did he care so strongly about the answers to his own questions?

As Cal put the tray down on the bedside table, she tried to struggle to an upright position, her lower lip clamped between her teeth. He'd been concussed once, on the Eiger, and it had left him with a splitting headache. He slid the pillows from behind her back, propping them against the headboard; then he put his hands under her armpits, lifting her whole weight.

The soft swell of her breast brushed his forearm, the contact surging through his body. Unceremoniously he pushed her back on the pillows, hearing her shallow, rapid breathing. He said with unwilling compassion, "I asked Maria for some painkillers, you'd better take one."

"They've probably got arsenic in them."

"I'll take one, too," he said dryly, "if that'll make you feel safer."

"I don't like taking pills."

"Is that how you got pregnant?"

He hadn't meant to ask that. He watched emotion rip across her face, raw agony, terrible in its intensity. As he instinctively reached out a hand in sympathy, she struck it away. "Just leave me alone," she cried. *"Please."*

She couldn't possibly have faked that emotion. The pain was real. All too real. He said flatly, "So you regret getting rid of the baby."

"Why don't you use the real word? Abortion. Because that's what you mean. And that's what Dieter and Maria think I did."

"That's certainly what they told me."

"And you believe everything you're told?"

"Why would they lie to me, Joanna?" Cal asked, and found he was holding his breath for the answer.

"Because no woman in the world would have been good enough for their beloved Gustave! I was their enemy from the very first day he brought me here."

Could it be true? Cal rested the tray on her lap and reached down to put more wood on the fire.

When he turned back, she was making a valiant effort to eat. But soon she pushed the bowl away. "That's enough," she mumbled, her lashes drifting to her cheeks.

He took the tray from her, standing by the bed until her breathing settled into the steady rhythms of sleep. She'd stopped shivering, and there was the faintest wash of color in her cheeks. She was going to be fine and he was a fool to stay in this room overnight. How could he lust after a woman whose every word he seemed to distrust?

First thing tomorrow he'd organize a tow truck and see her on her way. Then he'd give the Strassens Gustave's gear and head for the airport. They'd rebooked him on a flight midmorning. Twenty-four hours and he'd have seen the last of Joanna Strassen.

It couldn't be soon enough.

Glancing at his watch, Cal saw to his dismay that it was scarcely eight o'clock. After leaving the bedroom, he checked out the tidy ranks of books in the parlor. He'd been meaning to read the classics, and apparently now was the time for him to start, he thought wryly, leafing through a couple of volumes of Dickens. Then Dieter spoke from the doorway. "Ah, I thought I heard you in here. Maria and I are not our best, Cal, you must forgive us. You have no suitcase, nothing. Please let us give you a new toothbrush, some pajamas."

Cal never wore pajamas. "That's very kind of you."

"Come through to the kitchen, and I will get them for you."

Maria was putting away the dishes. Cal said pleasantly, "Your daughter-in-law has no nightclothes—could I trouble you for something?"

Her lips thinned. Without a word she left the room, returning with a carefully folded pair of striped pajamas over her arm. "Give her these."

"We'll be gone by morning," he said gently.

"I regret the day our son first saw those big blue eyes of hers!"

Dieter came through the door, passing Cal towels, pajamas and toilet articles. "Thank you," Cal said. "I'll say good night now, I'm a bit jet-lagged."

He was actually distressingly wide awake, all his nerves on edge. Grabbing *War and Peace* from the shelves on his way by, he strode to the back bedroom. Joanna was still sleeping, her neck crooked at an awkward angle. For several minutes he simply stared at her, as though the very stillness of her features might answer some of the questions that tumbled through his brain. She was too thin, he thought. Too pale. Asleep, she looked heartbreakingly vulnerable.

Normally he was a fairly astute judge of character. But something about Joanna had disrupted his radar. One thing he did know: next time he was asked to do a favor for a dead mountaineer, he'd run a mile in the opposite direction.

He added more wood to the fire and settled down with his book. Two hours later, adding one name to his handwritten chart of the characters, he realized the fire had nearly died out. After he'd added some kindling and a small log, he turned around to find Joanna Strassen's eyes open, fixed on him. They looked almost black, he thought. Depthless and mysterious. Full of secrets.

He said heartily, "Sorry if I woke you. How are you feeling?"

"I have to go to the bathroom."

Moving very carefully, she sat up. Then she swung her legs over the side of the bed and pushed herself upright. Abruptly she brought her hand to her forehead, staggering a little. "I feel so dizzy..."

"Here," Cal said unwillingly, "lean on me."

She swayed toward him. He put an arm around her waist, furious with himself for liking her height, and the way her cheek brushed his shoulder. "Why don't you have a hot bath?" he added noncommittally. "It would relax you."

She stopped, looking him full in the face. "I won't relax until I'm on a plane heading east," she muttered. Then her jaw dropped. "My flight—I've missed it!"

"Everything's canceled because of the storm."

Agitated, she said, "It was a seat sale, will they charge me more?"

Franz had said she was miserly with her money. Is that why she wore no jewelry? "They won't. But if they did, surely you could afford it?"

Her eyes suddenly blazed like blue fire. "Oh, of course. I'm a rich widow. How stupid of me to forget."

He'd always liked a woman with spirit. Suzanne, his

wife, had made a fine art out of avoiding conflict. But then Suzanne had had something perennially childlike about her; she'd never matched him, adult to adult. When he'd married her, he'd been too much in love to understand that about her; or to anticipate how her behavior would affect him.

Suzanne had also lied to him frequently, with casual expertise. He'd gradually come to understand that she didn't lie out of malice, but simply because it was easier than owning up to responsibilities or consequences; after a while he'd stopped expecting anything more from her than a modicum of truth. While he certainly was intelligent enough to realize that every beautiful woman wasn't necessarily a liar, Suzanne's legacy, overall, had been a deep-seated reluctance toward any kind of facile trust. This trait had done well for him in the world of business. But as far as Joanna was concerned, was it doing him a disservice?

With an effort Cal came back to the present. "Maria's loaned you something to wear to bed. I'll get it for you."

As she supported herself on the frame of the bathroom door, he passed her the pajamas. Automatically she took them, the fingers of her other hand digging into the wood; for a moment Cal wondered if she was going to faint. He grabbed her around the waist. "What's wrong?"

"How she hates me," Joanna whispered, and suddenly flung the pajamas to the floor. "Don't you see? They're Gustave's pajamas! She knew I'd recognize them."

Cal said evenly, "You hated Gustave. Didn't you?"

"I no longer loved him. If that's what you mean."

"I'm not sure it is."

"You won't believe me when I say this, because your mind's made up about me. But a long time ago I realized that to hate Gustave would destroy me."

Hate was horribly destructive: Cal was certainly sophisticated enough to know that. He said provocatively, "So you destroyed him instead?"

She sagged against the door frame. "Can one person destroy another? Doesn't destruction come from within?"

Again, Cal could only agree with her. Into his silence, Joanna added fiercely, "So you think I could destroy you? And how would I go about doing that?"

"Like this," said Cal, putting his arms around her and kissing her full on the mouth.

She went rigid with shock, her palms bunched into fists against his chest. Then she wrenched her head free, her breasts heaving under her sweater. "Tell the truth—it's you who wants to destroy me," she cried. "But I won't let you, I'll never let a man that close to me again."

What the devil had possessed him to kiss her like that? And why, when she was glaring at him as though he was the Marquis de Sade, did he want to kiss her again? But differently this time, not out of anger but out of desire.

The bruise on her forehead standing out lividly, she backed into the bathroom and slammed the door in his face. The lock snapped into place. If she'd taken the prize for stupidity by attempting to drive a small white car through a blizzard, he was now a close second. Kissing Joanna Strassen had been the stupidest move he'd made in a dog's age.

But he'd liked kissing her. More than liked it. It had inflamed every one of his senses.

When he left Winnipeg, he was headed to Boston on business. He'd give Jasmine a call. Wine her and dine her and take her to bed. That's what he'd do. And the sooner the better.

In fact, he might even phone her from here. Yeah, he might just do that.

Picking up Gustave's pajamas from the floor, Cal put them on the dresser. He could hear water running in the bathroom. He hoped to God Joanna wouldn't slip or faint in the bathtub.

He'd broken a car window already today. He could always break down the bathroom door.

That would really impress Maria.

Somewhat cheered, Cal picked up *War and Peace* again. He had the whole night. He might as well get on with it.

Half an hour later, Joanna opened the bathroom door. She was fully dressed, her cheeks pink from the heat. Cal said calmly, "You can have these," and passed her the new pajamas Dieter had given him.

"They're yours," she said inimically.

"They're Dieter's. I never wear pajamas."

"And where are you planning to sleep?" Her nostrils flared. "Do you know what? I don't even know your name."

"Cal," he said, and held out his hand, adding ironically, "Pleased to meet you."

She kept her own hands firmly at her sides. "Answer the question."

"On the couch. Unless you'd rather have it. It'll be too short for me."

"As far as I'm concerned you can sleep outdoors in a snowdrift."

For the first time since finding her in the car, Cal's smile broke through. "That's not very nice of you. I did, after all, save your life."

"And would you have, had you known who I was?"

"Of course I would. What kind of a question's that?"

She chewed on her lower lip. "Thank you," she said grudgingly. "I guess."

"Put on your pajamas and go to bed," Cal ordered. "Before you fall flat on your face."

She was scowling at him as though her one desire was to strangle him with the pajamas. Cal quelled an inappropriate urge to laugh his head off. He'd give her one thing: she sure didn't back down.

She shut the bathroom door smartly in his face. He remade the bed, stoked the fire, and went back to his book. Considering the disruptive effect a black-haired woman was having on his life, he was getting quite interested in the doings of Pierre, Natasha and Prince Andrew. He'd have to tell Lenny. She'd be impressed.

The door opened again. As Cal glanced up, *War and Peace* fell from the arm of his chair to the floor with a resounding thump. Dieter was a big man: his pajamas were far too large for Joanna. Even though she'd buttoned them to the very top, her cleavage was exposed, a soft shadow in the V of the neckline; the blue cotton hinted at her breasts. The sleeves fell over her fingertips, and she'd turned up the cuffs of the trousers. Cal found himself staring at her bare feet, which were narrow and high-arched. Then his eyes of their own accord found her face again.

She had freed her hair from its braid, so that it rippled down her back. Under his scrutiny, she was blushing as though she were as innocent as his own daughter.

Which, of course, she wasn't.

Slowly Cal got to his feet.

CHAPTER THREE

As JOANNA took a nervous step backward, Cal stopped dead in his tracks. He'd been going to kiss her again; that had been his intention. A repeat of a less than clever move.

He said roughly, "Will the light bother you if I read for a while?"

"No," she stumbled, "no, of course not."

"I'll probably wake you up a couple of times in the night—that's standard practice after a bump on the head."

"Oh." She swallowed, the muscles moving in her throat. "I don't think that's necessary, I feel much better."

"Let me be the judge of that."

For a moment he thought she was going to argue with him. But then the flare of temper died from her eyes. She got into bed, pulled the covers up to her chin and turned her back to him. Within a very few minutes, Cal could hear the gentle rhythm of her breathing, and realized he'd been reading the same paragraph over and over again.

Swearing under his breath, he forced himself to read on. Before he made up a bed on the couch at eleven-thirty, and again at two in the morning, he checked her pulse and the dilation of her pupils, both times without waking her. But at five, when the beam of his flashlight fell on her face, her eyes jerked open, full of terror. Like those of a rabbit who sights the talons of an owl seconds before they strike, Cal thought, and said with swift compassion, "It's okay, I'm just checking to see you're all right."

She sank back on the pillow, her pulse hammering at the base of her throat. "Is that the wind I hear?" she whispered.

"Yeah."

"I've got to get out of here today!"

"It'll die down soon," he said without much conviction; if anything, the storm had increased in intensity in the night.

"I can't stay here any longer."

She'd spoken in such a low voice he had to strain to hear her. She looked at the end of her tether, as though at the slightest provocation she would start to weep and be unable to stop. "I want to leave here, too," Cal said dryly. "But unfortunately neither one of us can influence the weather."

"To be here," she faltered, "don't you see, it brings it all back, all those terrible, wasted years. And the baby...I can't bear to think about the baby."

The fire had died down; he and Joanna were isolated in the small circle of his flashlight, darkness and the cry of the wind pressing in on all sides. Cal had never seen such desolation on a woman's face; it cut him to the heart. Clumsily he sat down on the bed and put his arms around her.

For a few seconds she yielded, her forehead burrowed in his shoulder, her spine a long curve of surrender. Through the thin cotton of his shirt, he felt tears dampen his skin, and realized she was weeping without a sound. "Did you really abort the baby?" he asked with sudden urgency.

"I didn't! I swear I didn't. It didn't matter that I no longer loved Gustave, I'd have loved the baby...I already did love it."

He wanted to believe her—God, how he wanted to! So what was holding him back?

Her hair smelled enticingly of hyacinths, and the soft weight of her breasts against his chest—bare where his shirt was open—filled Cal with a fierce surge of desire. He fought to subdue it. Was he about to take Gustave's widow to bed in Gustave's house? What kind of a man would that make him? In a harsh voice he scarcely recognized as his own, he said, "I don't know who the hell to believe—you or your dead husband's parents."

She flinched as though he'd physically struck her. Then she pulled free of him, swiping at the tears on her cheeks with the back of one hand. "You can keep your sympathy," she said stonily, "I as good as killed Gustave and I certainly killed the baby. Oh, and I was promiscuous, let's not forget that."

"I'm not sure sympathy's what this is about," said Cal, and kissed her hard on the mouth.

It was as though the flames suddenly rekindled in the hearth, lapping him in their fiery dance. He'd never felt such raw, basic hunger in his life. His arm tightened around her waist. Her ribs were a taut curve, her hair tumbling over the hand that was pressed to her back. Then her lips, warm and soft, yielded so suddenly and so ardently to his kiss that he'd have sworn she was enveloped in the same fire. He thrust with his tongue and fumbled for the buttons on her pajamas.

She struck him hard on his bare shoulder with her bunched fist and yanked her head free. "Don't!"

His arms aching with emptiness, Cal snarled with no subtlety whatsoever, "You kissed me back."

"All right, so I did. So what?"

"You've been widowed three months and you kissed me as though it's been three years."

"For the space of five seconds, I kissed you."

"Franz said you were promiscuous."

"Franz? I'd hardly call him a reliable witness."

She had a point, Cal thought reluctantly. He knew nothing about Franz. Had never met him before that day on Mont Blanc.

"Anyway," Joanna went on, "what about you? Why would you want to kiss me? You've made it all too clear you don't believe a word I've said. Which means you think I'm responsible for Gustave's death, and—'' momentarily she faltered ''—the loss of the baby, as well.''

Cal had no answer for her. When he was blinded by lust, how could he possibly discern the truth? But if he really did disbelieve her, he was kissing a woman he should despise.

He'd loved Suzanne when he married her, he'd never been unfaithful to her, and anyone he'd taken to his bed since her death he'd at least liked. He pushed himself up from the bed, noticing with one small part of his brain that Joanna's cheeks were still streaked with tears and that the bruise on her forehead was now a lurid mix of purple and yellow. ''Let's just call it temporary insanity,'' he said tersely. ''On both our parts.''

''It's not going to happen again!''

He could see the hard jut of her nipples beneath her jacket. ''You don't have a worry in the world,'' he grated. ''I'm going back to sleep. Alone. And we'd better hope the weather improves.''

''It's got to,'' she said with an edge of real desperation.

He felt exactly the same way. Although he was damned if he was going to tell her that. He'd already made enough of a fool of himself, no point in adding to it. ''Are you warm enough?'' he asked curtly.

''Yes. Thank you.''

He flicked off the flashlight and lowered his body onto a couch that was at least eight inches too short for him. He didn't care what the weather was doing, he was out of here once it was daylight. And he wasn't taking Joanna Strassen with him.

Daylight was chinking through the dark brown curtains when Joanna woke up. She lay still for a moment, totally disoriented, wondering why her head hurt and why the wind was howling so ferociously that the house creaked under its onslaught. Then it all came flooding back. Her disastrous and ill-thought-out attempt at reconciliation with Dieter and Maria. Her precipitate departure yesterday afternoon and the way the car had slid so gracefully and inevitably into the telephone pole. Her return to consciousness in this room, the waves of dizziness and pain, the gradual realization that she was back in the one place in the world she'd hoped never to see again.

And then there was her rescuer.

It wasn't chance that she'd left him to the last. Had she ever laid eyes on a man so magnetic, so masculine, so self-assured? So guarded, so reluctant to trust her? Why couldn't she have been rescued by a country farmer in a three-ton truck, with a plump, friendly wife and a kitchen smelling of borscht and freshly baked bread?

Cal was his name. And that was all she knew about him.

Except for the inescapable fact that his two brief kisses had melted the very bones of her body.

She had to get out of here. Soon. Sooner. Soonest.

Cautiously Joanna sat up. In the dim light, she could see Cal stretched out on the couch, his feet dangling over the edge, his neck stuck at an awkward angle. A blanket half covered his long body. He was still sound asleep.

He'd saved her life. If he hadn't come along, she'd have frozen to death.

She shivered, knowing that in spite of all the unhappiness of her marriage, and the acute pain of the last few months, she was deeply glad to be alive. So she had much to thank him for, this dark-haired stranger with eyes as gray and depthless as a winter sea.

If only he didn't share Dieter and Maria's opinion of her character. Which was, to put it mildly, rock-bottom. Why that should hurt her so badly, she didn't understand. He was a stranger, chance-met and soon to be forgotten. So why should it matter what he thought of her?

Not liking her own thoughts, Joanna got up as quietly as she could, parted the curtains and peered outside. Her heart sank. All she could see was the driven whiteness of snow; all she could hear was the howl of the wind. It was worse than yesterday, she thought numbly. But she had to leave. She had to.

From behind her Cal said with a lack of emotion that infuriated her, "Looks like we'll be stuck here today, too."

She whirled, frightened that she hadn't heard him get up, let alone cross the room. He was standing altogether too close, his crumpled shirt unbuttoned from throat to navel, his cords creased from sleeping in them. The sheen on his tousled hair reminded her of mahogany; her mother had left her a beautiful little mahogany end table. Then he yawned, and the corded muscles of his belly tightened; all his muscles were truly impressive, she thought wildly.

"I'm leaving here this morning," she spat. "You can do what you like."

"And how are you going to leave?" he said mockingly. "Your car's wedged to a telephone pole three miles down the road, and I'm not driving you anywhere, not in this." He lifted one brow. "Unless you think Dieter will lend you his car?"

So angry she could barely talk, she seethed, "I will not stay one more hour in a house where everyone—including you—thinks I'm a cold-blooded, immoral bitch!"

"I'm not—"

As if he hadn't spoken, she swept on, "I made the biggest mistake in my life—apart from marrying Gustave, that is—to fly out here with belongings of his I thought his parents should have. To believe that now he was dead, maybe we could somehow make peace. I sure go to the top of the class for naiveté."

"Naive isn't exactly the word I'd use for you."

"But you know nothing about me, Mr. Cal whatever-your-name-is. Only what you've been told. *You're* the one who's naive. You believe Dieter and Maria, who thought the universe revolved around Gustave. And you believe Franz, who hero-worshiped him and made one heck of a lot of money out of him into the bargain. Three cheers for you."

She was being very childish, she thought in a sudden wave of exhilaration. And it felt extremely good. She added peevishly, "What *is* your last name? And what are you doing here? You don't look the type to be a friend of the Strassens."

"Cal Freeman," Cal said, and watched her closely.

Her brow furrowed. "The name's familiar...but we've never met, I'd have remembered you."

"I'm a mountaineer."

She paled. "That's where I've heard your name—Franz was telling us once about the team you took up Everest."

"Franz gave me Gustave's climbing gear to bring to the Strassens."

She clutched the bedpost, her voice ragged. "Did you know Gustave?"

"No. But I'd heard of him, of course. I was sorry to hear he'd died."

"Play with fire," she said unsteadily, "and sooner or later you get burned."

The words were out before he could prevent them. "You being the fire?"

She raised her chin. "No, Cal. The mountains. The mountains that I grew to hate because they destroyed any chance I might have had of happiness."

"So you think all mountaineers are irresponsible dare-devils?"

"You're darn right I do."

He tapped himself on the chest. "Not this one."

Her eyes seemed to have glued themselves to the taut skin over his breastbone, with its tangle of dark hair. "Then you're the exception that proves the rule," she said, and couldn't have disguised the bitterness in her tone.

"Gustave was a mountaineer when you met him."

"And I was nineteen. Young enough to find both him and the mountains romantic."

It was an entirely plausible reply. Feeling frustrated and unsure of himself, Cal ventured, "You were jealous of the mountains?"

"I suppose I was," she said wearily. "Are you married, Cal? Does your wife hate it when the mountains take you away from her?"

Years ago, whenever Cal used to go on an expedition, Suzanne would fly to Paris and indulge in an orgy of shopping. He'd sometimes thought it would have suited Suzanne very well to have been left a wealthy widow; she'd have had the fun of spending his money without the bother of a relationship with a real, flesh-and-blood man. "That's none of your business," he said tersely.

"I beg your pardon," Joanna retorted. "So you can ask questions but I can't?"

Cal said impatiently, "I'm not spending the entire day trading insults with you."

"No, you're not. You're moving into the other part of the house, where you can spend the day with Dieter and Maria." With a flick of malice, Joanna added, "Have a good one."

Curiosity overcoming everything else, Cal asked, "Has this house always been so bleak and bare?"

"Ever since I've been coming here." Joanna bit her lip. "I'm sure it wasn't easy for Gustave, growing up with such strict, joyless parents. At first I tried to be understanding, but that wore thin after a while."

Wishing with fierce intensity that he'd just once met Gustave Strassen so he could have formed his own opinion of the man, and wishing with equal intensity that he could spend the entire day in bed with Gustave's widow, Cal said harshly, "If you'll excuse me I'm going to have a shower, get breakfast and check the weather report. Then I'll bring you something to eat."

"Bread and water?"

"Don't be ridiculous."

"It's not so ridiculous. Because I'm a prisoner in this room, aren't I?"

She was. No question of it. And he along with her. "Pray for sunshine," Cal said ironically, and headed for the bathroom.

It would have given Joanna enormous satisfaction to have thrown her pillow at his retreating back. Or drummed her heels on the cold hardwood and screamed out all her frustration. She did neither one. Cal Freeman already thought she was the equivalent of pond scum. A tantrum would really finish her off.

Why did she care what he thought?

So he had a great body. More than great, she thought, her mouth dry. And she'd be willing to bet he was quite unaware of the effect of his physique on a woman who, apart from that one time a few months ago, hadn't been to bed with anyone for at least four years. Including her lawfully wedded husband, Gustave Strassen.

Not that Cal would believe that.

Cal Freeman. She'd heard about him over the years. That spectacular ascent of the northeast ridge of Everest. His climbs on the Kishtwar range and the Kongur Massif. His heroic rescue of two French climbers in the Andes. Gustave had never encouraged talk about Cal Freeman; Gustave had always wanted to be the center of attention, another facet of his character that a love-blind nineteen-year-old had totally missed.

How ironic that Cal should have effected another rescue, this time of Gustave's widow, from a blizzard on the prairies.

Hurriedly Joanna got dressed; she was already heartily sick of her blue sweater. Then she braided her hair, made the bed, drew the curtains, and undid her briefcase. If she was to be stuck here for the morning—beyond the morning, she refused to look—she might as well get some work done.

So when Cal emerged from the bathroom, his hair still damp, she had her laptop set up and was frowning at the screen. He said, "I'll be back in half an hour with your breakfast."

She nodded without raising her eyes. He added, an edge of steel in his voice, "Where I come from, you look at someone when they speak to you."

"I'm working—can't you see?"

"According to Franz you've got lots of money. So what kind of work do you do that's so important that you can't even be civil?"

This time her head snapped up. "What I do with all the spare time I have as a stinkingly rich widow is none of your business."

"Don't push your luck, Joanna," Cal said with dangerous softness.

He hadn't yet shaved; the dark shadow on his jawline did indeed make him look dangerous. But Joanna had done a lot of growing up since she was nineteen. "And what happens if I do?"

"I wouldn't advise you to ask that question unless you're prepared for the answer."

Although her pulse was beating uncomfortably fast, she said with credible calm, "He-man stuff."

His words had an explosive force. "Do you have any idea how beautiful you are? Especially when you're in a rage."

A blush scorched her cheeks. "Don't change the subject!"

"Oh, I don't think I am." He gave her a grin she could only call predatory. "I'll be back."

The bedroom door closed behind him. Joanna let out her breath in a long sigh. She wasn't normally argumentative, nor was she overly aware of the male half of the species: if Gustave had been anything to go by, she was better off alone. But Cal Freeman seemed to destroy all the self-sufficiency she'd striven to achieve over the long years of her marriage.

Her first resolution, she thought fiercely, was to work all morning. And her second, to ignore the dark-haired man who was virtually her jailer.

She turned her attention back to the screen, and by sheer stubbornness managed to immerse herself in revising the tenth chapter. Her New York agent had already found a publisher for this, her second novel; she was determined it wasn't going to bomb, as could so often happen with second novels. Especially after all the critical attention the first one had gained.

It seemed no time before Cal opened the door, carrying a tray. Quickly she closed the file; she had no intention of him finding out about her other life as a writer. She said casually, "That smells good."

"I cooked the eggs myself," Cal said. "Didn't want Maria pouring hot pepper sauce all over them."

She steeled herself against the laughter lurking in his gray eyes. "What's the weather forecast?"

"Like this all day. Wind dying around midnight, the plow should come through during the night, and I've booked a tow truck first thing tomorrow. No flights out of Winnipeg today.''

''Oh, that's just wonderful,'' said Joanna, fighting down a wave of panic that was out of all proportion.

Cal's eyes narrowed. ''I'm going out to my vehicle to bring in Gustave's gear,'' he said coldly. ''I'm presuming you don't want any of it?''

She flinched. ''No,'' she said in a low voice. ''I don't need a harness or a set of ropes to remind me of Gustave.''

Cal plunked the tray down on the table. The trouble was, she fascinated him with far more than her incredible beauty. Anger, sadness, frustration, terror, she'd shown them all; and now he had to add a kind of dignity that he could only respect. ''Eat your breakfast,'' he ordered. ''Any complaints about the eggs can be directed to the chef.''

She suddenly grinned. ''I'm hungry enough they could be as tough as climbing boots and I wouldn't complain.''

Her smile was full of mischief. Turning away so he wouldn't grab her with all the subtlety of a caveman, Cal said brusquely, ''I'll be back with your lunch.'' Then he wheeled and left the room.

The next couple of hours were far from pleasant for Cal. Maria's iron façade wasn't equal to seeing her son's climbing gear; Dieter openly had tears in his eyes. Against his will, Cal's anger toward Joanna was revived; although he was honest enough to admit some of that anger should be directed toward himself for letting her get past his defences so easily. Eventually the Strassens disappeared to their own room; around noon, his eyes tiring from the fine print of *War and Peace,* Cal took himself to the kitchen and produced some untidy but interesting sandwiches for himself and Joanna. Picking up hers, he headed back to the bedroom.

He could be very soft-footed when he chose to be. Not

stopping to analyze just why he should want to take Joanna by surprise, Cal padded into the bedroom they'd shared last night. She was scowling into her laptop computer, totally focused on what she was doing. He couldn't help admiring her concentration, for Joanna Strassen definitely didn't want to be here: that much he did believe. Suzanne, under similar circumstances, would have been indulging in a major sulk. But Joanna was being…stoic, he thought. Stoicism was right up there in his list of virtues.

She'd fastened her hair in an untidy mass on top of her head; skewering the shiny black coils was a yellow pencil. As he watched, she leafed through a black-covered journal to her left, read half a page intently, and began rummaging through the papers on the table, muttering something under her breath.

Cal said lightly, "What's your problem?"

She jumped, knocking several papers to the floor. "Do you get a kick out of creeping up on people?" she demanded. "Where the *hell* is my pencil?"

"In your hair," he said amiably.

Her scowl deepened. "I've been doing that for years—I never think to look there and don't you dare laugh at me." Her gaze dropped to the plate in his hands. "You expect me to eat those?"

He glanced down. The tomato slices had skidded, the lettuce was falling out, and he'd been so generous with the egg salad that each sandwich bulged bounteously. Like a pregnant woman, he thought. "I couldn't care less if you eat them or not! After Dieter and Maria saw Gustave's gear they were very upset, and I sure as heck wasn't going to ask either one of them to make your lunch."

Joanna pushed back her chair, stood up and marched over to him. Her chin high, she said, "I'm sorry they've lost their son. Truly I am. But Gustave was a disaster wait-

ing to happen—far too taken up with his own ego to be
half the climber they thought he was.''

''If he'd just found out you were pregnant and he wasn't
sure who'd fathered the child—that's completely irrele-
vant?''

''He knew who the father was. Trust me.''

Why couldn't he trust her? She wasn't Suzanne: or even
remotely like Suzanne. Deliberately needling her, Cal said,
''How could he have known? There are a lot of men in
Europe.''

''And according to Dieter and Maria I've slept with most
of them.'' She gave an unamused laugh. ''I'd like to know
when I'd have found the time.''

Suzanne still on his mind, Cal said with a touch of bitterness, ''Some women can always find time for what they
want to do.''

Joanna said very softly, ''Why don't you stick to stuff
you know something about? Because you know what? I
hate generalizations almost as much as I hate false accusations.'' Putting her head to one side, she examined him
with a clinical detachment Cal thoroughly disliked. ''Oddly
enough, I'd have thought you were too intelligent for either
one.''

Normally, Cal would have thought the same thing.
Pushing his luck, he said, ''So whose baby was it,
Joanna?''

''Gustave's. Of course.''

Of course. Cal dumped the tray on the coffee table. ''I'll
bring you dinner around six-thirty,'' he muttered, and
marched out of the room to find his book. The fact that
Joanna was every bit as complex as some of the characters
both incensed and confused him. For a man who'd made
his first fortune by the time he was twenty-three, he was
behaving like an idiot. A total Neanderthal.

Going back into the kitchen, Cal picked up his own sandwiches, sat down in the bleak parlor, and opened *War and Peace*. He wasn't going to think about Joanna Strassen until suppertime.

Not once.

CHAPTER FOUR

JOANNA ate her sandwiches, which were as tasty as they were messy, did some energetic stretches, and saw with true despair that somehow these two tasks had only passed thirty-nine minutes. Had a day ever been so interminable? Had she ever wished so passionately to be elsewhere?

She picked up her pile of papers, forcing herself to enter that other world of the imagination; and hour by slow hour the afternoon passed. But by six o'clock Joanna was desperate to escape the confines of the bedroom. She marched up and down, counting the turns under her breath, pumping her arms vigorously. She should exercise more often; she hadn't really regained her strength since losing the baby.

Her eyes filmed with tears. Joanna scrubbed them away. The past was over. Over and done with. Tomorrow when she left here, she must put it behind her. She had a teaching job that paid the bills, she had her all-important vocation as a writer, and she had two good friends back home in the little university town of Harcourt, Nova Scotia. She was extraordinarily lucky.

As she blinked the last tears away, Joanna became aware that for the past few minutes a man had been speaking on the other side of the closed bedroom door. Cal. She'd know his voice anywhere. She crept closer to the door, unashamedly listening. He was on the phone, she realized, and strained to hear.

"I'm glad we've been able to talk," he was saying, "whatever did people do before long distance? And of course I want you to be happy...no, I'll be going on to New York, there's an auction of Chinese jade there next week…I know, darling, I know. But it's not much longer and then we can be together in the summer…okay, you'd better go. I'll call you tomorrow when I get to Boston. See you soon, sweetheart. 'Bye.''

The receiver was replaced with a soft click. Joanna straightened, her heart thumping. So Cal Freeman was either married or otherwise taken; and the woman in question was unhappy without him. Yet the only time he was willing to spend with her was the summer. Were all mountaineers the same? Demanding untrammeled freedom, but at the same time wanting the little woman to keep the home fires burning?

How his voice had softened when he'd called her *sweetheart*. Almost as though he'd meant it, Joanna thought cynically. Because this was the man who'd kissed her, Joanna, as though she were the only woman left on the surface of the earth.

Another man who believed words were as disposable as empty oxygen tanks. Worse, another mountaineer whose middle name was infidelity.

Who *was* the unknown woman he'd been talking to? Was she beautiful? Was she his wife? Or his mistress?

Then another voice spoke in the narrow hallway. ''Ah…there you are, Cal. Maria is making dinner, she's feeling a little better now. Why don't you join me for a drink? And tonight you must sleep in the guest room, you'll be much more comfortable there.''

''I would certainly prefer that,'' Cal said loudly, so loudly that Joanna shrank back, her cheeks hot. He couldn't have known she was listening…could he?

''Did you get your connection without any trouble?''

''Yes, thanks. Clear as a bell. It's so important to keep in touch, isn't it, when you—''

His voice was suddenly muffled as the door to the main house swung shut. Joanna wandered over to the window, staring into the snow and the endless darkness. There was no reason for her to feel so suddenly, acutely and miserably lonely. No reason at all.

Joanna woke early. She lay very still and realized she was listening to silence: the wind had died. She sprang out of bed and pulled back the curtains on a world of sculpted snowbanks and fading stars in the vastness of a prairie sky.

She could leave today. Leave and never come back.

For a moment she rested her forehead against the cold glass. Maybe coming here hadn't been such a terrible mistake, after all...for hadn't she, in the past couple of days, somehow severed the last of her ties to Gustave? Hopefully he really was part of her past now, this man she had once passionately loved; and it was in the past that he must remain.

Quickly she showered, toweled her hair dry and dressed. Then she closed her mind to everything but chapter eleven, and got to work. An hour later, Cal tapped on the door. "Are you awake, Joanna?"

"Come in," she said crisply.

He was wearing the same heavy sweater and thick cords; his hair shone with cleanliness, and he was clean-shaven. The cold white light from the window threw shadows over the jut of his cheekbones and the strong line of his jaw; his eyes were an unfathomable gray. Power was what he exuded, she decided, her mouth suddenly dry. The power of a man who'd met challenges that would have defeated a lesser man; the power of a man used to command. Certainly his masculinity would never be called into question. Sexy didn't even begin to describe him.

"Why are you staring at me?" he demanded.

"Trying to figure out what makes you tick."

The last thirty-six hours had disabused Cal of any notions

that he knew what made him tick. "You can keep your pretty nose out of my business," he retorted.

"Good morning to you, too," she said cordially.

He jammed his hands in his pockets. "The road's ploughed, and the tow truck's taking your car back to the airport...you managed to damage the radiator, so you can't drive it. Anyway, it's full of snow because I had to break one of the windows. The driver will leave your suitcase with the rental agency."

"It's only a small overnight bag," Joanna said, biting her lip. She had no idea what a tow truck cost, but she was willing to bet it wouldn't come cheap. With luck she could squeeze the bill onto her Visa and stay under her limit. But the insurance she'd purchased on the car was five-hundred-dollar deductible, she realized with a cold sinking in the pit of her stomach.

"What's the matter?" Cal rasped.

She blurted, "How much does a tow truck cost?"

"A couple of hundred, probably."

She'd definitely be over her limit. But there was about four hundred in her savings account, she could access that at the airport. Then she realized Cal was speaking again. "Sorry?" she muttered.

"Supposedly you've got lots of money."

"Suppositions can lead you badly astray."

"Supposedly you were too cheap to buy proper equipment for Gustave. Which supposedly had something to do with what happened on Annapurna."

Enough, thought Joanna in a flood of pure rage. More than enough. In fact, a great deal more than enough. "Just you listen to me, Cal Freeman! I had money when I married Gustave, quite a lot of money. He spent it, every single cent, going to the Alps and the Andes and Nepal and China. Plus he spent it on women, don't let's forget that—so many women I lost track. And I was too stupid, too trusting, too naive, to realize what he was doing until it was too late. Yes, he had second-rate equipment by the end. But that wasn't my fault, it was his. *His,* do you hear me?''

"I should think Maria and Dieter can hear you,'' Cal said in a peculiar voice. "Are you trying to tell me you're broke?''

"That's precisely what I'm telling you. That, and the simple fact that I'm sick to death of being accused of causing my husband's death.'' Her voice suddenly cracked. "My husband's and my unborn child's.''

She swung around to face the window, furious with herself for crying and too proud to let Cal see the tears trickling down her cheeks. Then she felt his hand fall heavy and warm on her shoulder. She whirled, striking it off, her eyes blazing. "Don't you dare touch me!''

"Don't cry, Joanna...please,'' Cal said, a note in his voice that was new to her.

"I'll cry if I want to,'' she retorted and made a dive for the box of tissues on the table. She blew her nose hard. Tears or no, she felt better right now than she'd felt since she arrived here two days ago. She'd been behaving with entirely too much restraint; losing her temper had felt just fine. And if Mr. Cal-Almighty-Freeman didn't like it, too bad.

"Either you're telling the truth, or you're an extremely good actress,'' Cal said slowly.

"Oh, in between my affairs with all the men in Europe, I went to drama school—did I forget to mention that?''

"They hate you, Dieter and Maria.''

"They hate life,'' she said pithily. "Life, laughter, fun, passion, red roses and sunsets—you've seen their house and don't get me going.''

"They loved their son.''

"Love's a word capable of many interpretations. Surely you're old enough and savvy enough to have learned that.

Not, of course, that I'm interested in your thought processes.''

"Did you ever love your husband?" Cal asked in the same infuriatingly level voice.

"Falling in love with Gustave was the biggest mistake of my whole life," she snapped, adding with complete untruth, "Look, Cal, I don't care whether you believe one word I've said to you or not. What I do care about is whether you'll drive me to the airport—or do I have to call a cab?"

"I'll drive you. We'll leave in half an hour. I'll bring you something to eat right away."

He turned on his heel and left the room. Joanna sagged into the nearest chair. Losing her temper had felt wonderful in the moment, she thought ruefully, but it had sure taken the good out of her. And it hadn't accomplished anything. Cal, she was almost sure, still didn't believe one word she'd said.

Which hurt. Rather a lot.

Cal pulled up outside the terminal building. "I'll leave you here and park in the rental area. See you in a few minutes."

"Fine," Joanna said briefly. For the past two hours, neither she nor Cal had said anything beyond commonplaces. She hurried inside the terminal, dismayed to see the crowds of delayed passengers and the length of the lineups. She had to get out of here today. She couldn't afford a night in a hotel.

Planting herself at the end of the line, she took out a paperback novel. Half an hour passed, during which she shuffled in small stages closer to the counter. Then from the corner of her eye she saw Cal duck under the tape. She closed her book. How appropriate that they say goodbye here in a crowd of strangers, she thought. For hadn't each of them remained a stranger to the other?

Cal said curtly, "I'm on a flight to Boston that leaves in an hour, I was lucky to get it."

Boston. The woman he'd called *sweetheart*, hadn't he said he'd phone her from Boston? Was that where she lived?

"Where are you headed?" Cal finished.

Joanna clutched her book to her chest; she was using her ticket as a bookmark. "I reckon I'll go to Hawaii—spend some more of my money."

"Where do you live, Joanna?"

"You don't need to know that."

"For some reason that escapes me," he said in a savage whisper, "I do."

"Too bad."

"In that case I guess I'll just have to stay by your side all the way to the counter."

"Cal," she seethed, "go to Boston. Go to hell for all I care. After today we'll never see each other again—and never's too soon for me. In other words, get lost!"

"I don't think I'm quite ready to do that."

She couldn't lose her temper again. Not twice in one day. The woman ahead of her was listening with unabashed interest, and the couple behind her, who'd been bickering ever since they'd joined the lineup, had fallen silent. To get a lesson from the professionals, Joanna thought wryly. And would it really matter if Cal found out she was flying to Halifax? She didn't live there, and she certainly wasn't going to give him her address. "Do what you like," she said with assumed indifference. "I'd hate for you to miss your plane, though."

"You let me worry about that."

Ostentatiously she reopened her book and began to read; and in fifteen minutes, with Cal so close to her the elusive tang of his aftershave teased her nostrils, she reached the counter. "Halifax?" the man said, and consulted his computer. "First flight I can get you on is at three-thirty, via Toronto, getting into Halifax at seven forty-six."

Joanna gave him a brilliant smile. No hotel. No more bills added to her overloaded credit card. "That's wonderful, thank you," she said, and a few minutes later had her boarding card. She marched away from the lineup, glanced at her watch and said levelly to the man glued to her side, "You'd better go through security—they won't wait for you."

Cal pulled a piece of paper from his pocket and thrust it between the pages of her book. Then he took her by the shoulders, his fingers digging through her coat. "I've given you a phone number where I can always be reached, plus my e-mail address." He hesitated, then went on with a raw honesty that took her aback, "I know this makes no sense, Joanna...but please give me your address. We're not finished with each other and don't ask me to explain that because I can't."

"You're wrong and the answer's no."

"We met under the worst of circumstances, and initially I had no reason to disbelieve Franz, or Dieter and Maria."

"Why don't you try believing me?"

Cal winced. Suzanne had spoken just like that after any number of escapades. And of course he'd learned not to believe her.

He'd hesitated too long. Joanna said coldly, "Go catch your plane. Why would I want to keep in touch with someone who thinks I've done nothing but lie to him since we met? You're really no different from Gustave's parents."

"You sure know how to flatter a guy."

Her question came from nowhere. "Cal, are you married?"

"No," he said curtly.

So the woman on the phone was his mistress. But a man wasn't labeled promiscuous if he had more than one woman on the go. No, he was admired. He was envied, not despised.

Joanna took a deep breath. "I know you saved my life—if you hadn't come along, I'd have frozen to death. I haven't really thanked you for that." She looked him right in the eye. "I do thank you. From the bottom of my heart. But as for the rest, we have nothing to say to each other."

"Then let me at least say this," he grated. Before she realized his intention, he slid his arms around her, pulled her hard against the length of his body, and kissed her with passionate intensity.

For a few seconds Joanna was so shocked that she was rigid in his embrace. But the heat of his lips, the sureness with which he moved his mouth against hers, the first thrust of his tongue, made her head swim and her body spring to life. She clutched his sleeves so she wouldn't fall, and kissed him back as though she'd never kissed a man in her life before, as though he were the first and she as innocent as a virgin.

Her pulse was racing; her breasts were pressed hard against his chest, and even through her coat she could feel his arousal. Desire, that had lain dormant in her for so many years, unfurled like the petals of a flower, encompassing her in the fiery beauty of her body's truth. She wanted Cal. Wanted him fiercely, urgently and now.

As she opened to him, her tongue meeting his with unbridled generosity, he strained her closer. His kiss deepened, until she swore she could feel the pounding of his heart in the thrumming of her own blood. It was a kiss she wanted to last forever, she thought dazedly, twining her arms around his neck, discovering with a small leap of surprise the warmth of his nape, the thick silkiness of his hair. From a long way away she heard a raucous laugh. Closer, a woman's voice said, "Oh, Mabel, aren't they cute?"

"Just like in the movies," the unknown Mabel breathed. "Airports are such fun, you never know what you're going to see next."

Cute, thought Joanna dimly. *Cute?*

Then Cal pushed her away so suddenly that she staggered. His chest heaving, he said in a voice she'd never heard him use before, "For someone who hates making a spectacle of himself, I seem to be excelling myself. Goodbye, Joanna Strassen. Don't spend all your money in Hawaii, will you?"

"I won't. And I'll only have affairs with half the men there," she said faintly, and watched him wheel and stride toward the escalator that led to security. A tall, broad-shouldered man wearing a down parka. A man who with one kiss had made nonsense of the celibacy she'd lived with for so long.

A man who couldn't decide whether she was telling the truth or acting her head off. Who had a mistress he called *sweetheart.*

A man she was never going to see again.

Thank heavens she hadn't given him her address. Because she couldn't afford to see him again. One more unfaithful mountaineer in her life would be one too many.

Her nose in the air, Joanna walked past Mabel and her friend, both of whom had blue rinses and were smiling at her with misty sentimentality. The rental agency was at the other end of the airport. She headed in that direction, clutching her paperback to her chest. Dealing with a broken radiator, a smashed window and a tow truck would bring her back to earth in a hurry.

A good thing, too.

CHAPTER FIVE

A STUPENDOUS view, a full stomach, and the company of
a good friend: what more could a man want?

He could want Joanna Strassen, thought Cal grimly.

Four months since he'd seen her and he still couldn't get
her out of his mind. Wasn't she the reason he was here,
sitting on the front deck of Ludo Galliker's chalet, which
faced the three snow-draped peaks of the Eiger, the
Mettenberg and the Wetterhorn, along with their mighty
glaciers? His old friend Ludo, retired now from guiding
groups up these same peaks, from whom he, Cal, had
learned so many of the basics all those years ago.

He'd driven the crowded highways from Lenny's school
near St. Gallen all the way to the tourist trap of Grindelwald
just to see Ludo. For old times' sake, certainly. But also to
ask him a question. A crucially important question.

Ludo came out on the deck, bearing a carved antique
tray on which was a full bottle of plum brandy and two
small glasses. He glanced over at the peaks, which the setting sun had tinged with rose. "Many years have gone by
since our first abseil on the Eiger," he said. "Do you remember the first time your father brought you here? What
were you, fourteen? But even then, strong as a man and
oh, so determined." He chuckled. "Not for you the easy
routes, the safe ones."

For a couple of hours, as the light faded from the meadows around the chalet and the level of brandy slowly sank
in the bottle, the two men reminisced about some of their
favorite climbs. Because Ludo was one of the few people
who had known Cal's flamboyant, affectionate father, Cal

always enjoyed these visits, and now felt a twinge of conscience that he hadn't come here more often: Ludo wasn't
getting any younger.

Not that Ludo would ever admit that. His shock of white
hair seemed imbued with its own energy, and his laugh was
as robust as ever. But Cal had noticed each time Ludo
lowered himself into his wooden chair, he'd moved carefully; his weathered hands were knotted with arthritis.

The first stars pierced the alpine sky. Into a gap in the
conversation, Cal said casually, "Did you ever come across
a climber called Gustave Strassen, Ludo?"

Ludo drained his glass, and refilled it. "Why do you
ask?"

"A few months ago, I met his widow."

"Ah...I, too, met her. Twice, some years ago. What did
you think of her?"

"I asked you about her husband. Not about her."

"So you did. Humor an old man, Cal. Give me your
impressions of Joanna Strassen."

Ludo's homemade brandy had defeated more than one
seasoned mountaineer; Cal said indiscreetly, "So beautiful
I can't get her out of my mind."

"So bedworthy, you mean?" Ludo said dryly.

"That, too. But not just that. Intelligent, fiery-tempered.
Yet according to Gustave's parents, she has the morals of
an alley cat."

"An alley cat? What does that mean?"

"Sleeps around," Cal said pungently.

Ludo delicately raised one brow. "So did she or didn't
she get into *your* bed?"

"Didn't," Cal exploded, "and what the devil's the al-
cohol content of this stuff we're drinking?"

"My secret," Ludo said with a smug smile. "Tell me
how you met her."

Briefly Cal described his errand to the prairies, the storm, the car in the ditch. "A guide I met on Mont Blanc said she denied her husband equipment that might have saved his life, and that she cheated on Gustave for years. Then, according to Gustave's parents, after he died she even aborted a child that might have been his," he finished, and heard pain underlying the anger in his voice.

Since last January, he'd done his level best to forget Joanna Strassen. He'd dated Jasmine in Boston, taking her for a very expensive dinner and then leaving her—to their mutual surprise—at the door of her condo. He'd dated women in New York, London and Zurich, beautiful, intelligent women who'd left him stone-cold. He'd led an expedition to Patagonia in March. He'd visited Lenny in February, April, and May, yesterday attending a performance of her school play. And none of it had worked. A tall, enigmatic woman with a sheaf of blue-black hair and eyes the vivid blue of delphiniums had haunted him, day and night. Although the nights, he admitted savagely, were the worst. By far.

Ludo said matter-of-factly, "And you believed these people? Gustave's parents and the guide?"

"At first I did. Why wouldn't I?"

"Even after you'd spent some time with Joanna, you still believed them?"

"I don't know!" Cal exclaimed in utter frustration. "I wanted to believe her, you don't know how I wanted to. But from the first moment I saw her, she knocked me right off balance—I didn't know which way was up."

Ludo raised his brows. "How about listening to a different version? That Gustave cheated on Joanna. That he spent her money as though it were water in a mountain stream, never to run dry. That he had an ego as big as the Eiger, a heart cold as the Aletsch glacier."

"And whose version is that?" Cal said carefully, noticing that his fingers weren't quite steady as he put his glass down on the tray.

"My version. And you know me for an honest man."

"You knew Gustave?"

"I came across him eight years ago when he was newly married, him and his beautiful wife. Because you are right, she is beautiful beyond any words that I could find. And, in those days, so in love, so blind to the man Gustave really was, that it hurt me to see it."

Cal poured himself another glass of *Pflümli*. He wasn't going anywhere tonight, and if he had the granddaddy of all hangovers tomorrow, that was the least of his worries. "You're saying the fault was all Gustave's?"

"Yes. I met them again, five years ago, at the cheese festival in the Justistal valley. She was trying to behave as though nothing was wrong; he was throwing his weight around, flirting with anything in skirts, and, according to report, bedding any who were willing. He was a bad man, Cal. And not even a very good climber. What saved him all those years were the guides he chose. He paid them well—from Joanna's money—and depended on them to keep him out of trouble. I, for one, wasn't surprised when he fell on Annapurna. Only surprised it had taken that long."

Cal said quietly, "My God…she'll never forgive me."

"For believing what everyone else told you about her?"

"Believing it. Throwing it in her face. Refusing to admit the evidence that was in front of my eyes that she was different."

"If you're in Grindelwald and she's in Canada, it will certainly be difficult for her to forgive you."

"If she were standing right here in front of me, she wouldn't forgive me."

"The first step is to ask her for forgiveness."

"Canada's a big country and I don't even know where she lives."

"I'm sure if you can track down a Vermeer that's been lost for three hundred years for one of your auctions, you can find this one woman," Ludo said with heavy irony.

"You think she'll talk to me after all the things I said?" Cal demanded in a cracked voice.

"Why is Lenny going to school in Switzerland, Cal?"

His brain whirling, Cal stared at his old friend. "What's that got to do with Joanna Strassen?"

"Answer the question."

"I thought it best for her. I'm away a fair bit, she's thirteen and needs female company—"

"She needs a mother."

"You can't just order one of those whenever it suits you!"

"Go and find Joanna Strassen. Lenny doesn't like her new school, you told me that while we were eating dinner."

"She's homesick. She'll settle down."

"You're paying huge fees at this so-elegant school so you can shirk your responsibilities to your daughter."

Cal said tightly, "Go easy, Ludo."

"You're in love with Joanna Strassen."

"Dammit, I'm not!"

"I think you are. I've known you for years and your father before you. He was a one-woman man—never looked at anyone else after your mother died. And you're the same. It's just that you've never found the right woman. You might have thought Suzanne was the one for you— but I knew better. Suzanne wasn't in any way a match for you. But Joanna—ah, Joanna Strassen is more than your match."

"Joanna Strassen thinks I'm worse than the dirt under her feet. And with good reason."

"Then you'll have to change her mind, won't you?"

"Are you saying I should *marry* her?"

"I do believe I am…I think a little chestnut torte would go well with the last of the brandy, what do you think?"

Cal rested his forehead on his hands. "It's true, isn't it? She never cheated on Gustave. I think part of me knew that all along."

"Never. I would swear to that in a court of law."

"So it must have been his child she was carrying. She told me she loved her unborn baby…so what happened to it?"

"I don't know the answer to that question. So why don't you ask her? She's the one who knows."

"Yeah," said Cal. "Just like that. You might as well suggest we scale the Matterhorn before breakfast."

With a heartless laugh Ludo levered himself up from his chair. "But you've always loved a challenge, haven't you?"

He'd rather climb the Matterhorn, before or after breakfast, than face Joanna Strassen, thought Cal. He knew where he was on the Matterhorn. Knew the dangers. A woman like Joanna was unknown territory.

She'd been faithful to her husband through the most difficult of marriages. Faithful to Gustave and truthful to Cal.

Somehow he had to find her. Find her, ask her to forgive him, and take her to bed.

And if that wasn't a challenge, he didn't know what was.

But marry her? What would he do that for? Because Ludo was wrong. Dead wrong. He, Cal, wasn't in love with Joanna Strassen.

No way.

"Apple tree," Joanna said slowly, standing under a haze of sweetly scented pink blossoms. "The apple tree is in bloom."

The small crowd of students surrounding her dutifully

stared up at the tree, which was loud with the buzzing of bees. "Apples," Luis said. "No apples. Not yet no apples."

"Not yet any apples," Joanna smiled. "In the autumn, there will be many apples on the tree. Do you understand, Luis?"

"In spring the tree is very beautiful," Sanches said, his voice without expression.

Joanna smothered a sigh. Sanches had the best grasp of English of all her foreign students, and not a scrap of poetry in his soul.

"Exquisito," said Angelica, *"sí perfumado."*

"Exquisite," Joanna responded, "so fragrant."

"Fray-grant," Angelica repeated, inhaling the scent of the clustered petals with a beatific smile.

They were grouped on the slope in front of the arts building on a sunny afternoon in early June; whenever possible, Joanna conducted her classes outdoors. Harcourt, in Nova Scotia's Annapolis Valley, was at its best in June: the fresh green leaves, the blossoming orchards, the birds in their bright plumage flitting among the trees.

It beat the prairies in January.

She didn't want to think about the prairies. In January or in June. She hadn't heard a word from Gustave's parents, not that she'd expected to. As for Cal Freeman, she'd forgotten him.

Or, to be more truthful, she wished she had.

"Bzzz?" said Rodrigo, and flapped his arms.

"Bee," Joanna said. "Bumblebee. Oh, and look, a bird in the branches of the tree...*un pájaro en las ramas de los arboles.*"

They were wandering in the general direction of the parking lot, where her plan was to talk about cars. Absently she noticed a bright red minivan pull into the lot allocated to the registrar; she'd had dinner with the registrar a couple of times recently, it was funny he hadn't mentioned he was buying such a splashy new vehicle.

Not that she'd encouraged him to confide in her. Even though he was a nice man. A very nice man, compared to Cal. She heaved a sigh. She'd really only gone out with the registrar because her two best friends, Sally and Dianne, were insistent she have some kind of social life that included the male of the species.

She didn't need men. Sally and Dianne were mistaken.

And then a man climbed out of the front seat of the minivan, and her heart lurched in her breast. It wasn't the registrar. It was Cal. Cal Freeman.

But it couldn't be. Not here. Just because she'd had some of the most graphic and erotic dreams in her life about that particular male didn't mean he was in Nova Scotia, walking across the grass toward her.

"The bird is yellow," said Sanches. "The bird sings."

"Canary," Luis said triumphantly.

Dazedly Joanna dragged her eyes away from the man, who was undoubtedly Cal Freeman. The bird was a gold-finch. "Not a canary," she stumbled, "we don't have wild canaries here."

"A man walks by the grass," Angelica said, giving Cal a thoughtful glance.

"Across the grass," Joanna corrected automatically, and made a valiant effort to pull herself together. "I don't want to talk to him, I'll send him away."

"Tall," said Angelica, smoothing her jet-black hair. "And very...*guapo*, how do you say in English?"

"Handsome," Sanches supplied.

"*Por Dios*, why you send him away?" Angelica asked.

Cal was now within earshot, Joanna realized, her mouth dry. He looked wonderful, his loose-limbed stride, his powerful shoulders and flat belly, the sun caught in his thick, dark hair. He was smiling at her. Smiling as if no one else in the world existed but her.

As though this were all happening to another woman, she watched him close the distance between them, his eyes pinioning her to the spot. Then he put his arms around her and kissed her full on the mouth.

Nothing had changed. Absolutely nothing. She still wanted him with every fiber of her being; and fought against a response as inevitable as the unfolding of apple blossoms to the heat of the sun. She jammed her fists against his chest and shoved hard, pulling her mouth free at the same time. "Stop it!" she gasped. "Can't you see I'm teaching?"

Cal looked around with leisurely interest. Angelica visibly preened, Luis gave him a comradely grin, while Sanches regarded him with the detached curiosity of a scientist examining a laboratory specimen. "And what are you teaching, Joanna, my darling?"

"I am not your darling! I'm teaching English as a second language and will you please leave immediately."

Ignoring this in a way that infuriated her, Cal said, "Are you explaining the beauties of springtime to them?"

"I was. Until you came along."

"Then let's give the lesson a boost," he said, smiling at her with such warmth that her heart flipped in her breast. "You look quite astonishingly beautiful, by the way." He glanced around. *"Bella. Muy bella."*

Blushing fierily, Joanna scowled at him. She was wearing purple walking shorts, a crisp white shirt with the sleeves rolled up, and thin-strapped sandals. She'd gained a little weight the last few months, and because she'd planted a garden at her rented cottage, her face and legs were lightly tanned. Then Cal reached over and plucked the pencil from her hair, which she'd gathered in a loose knot on her crown. "So you still do that," he said softly. "I don't think I've forgotten anything you did or said the whole time we spent together.''

Joanna finally found her voice. "Cal," she said strongly, "I haven't forgotten anything you said, either. Which is why I'm not falling into your arms, surprise, surprise. And now I have a job to do. Vamoose. Get lost. Take a hike. Go!''

"Get lost?" Luis repeated, puzzled, looking at the broad expanse of clipped lawn. "Here *es difícil* to be lost, no?''

"She means she'd like me to fall off the tip of the Matterhorn," Cal explained with a fiendish grin. "But, Joanna, *querida*, you can't have a lesson about springtime without including *amor. Te quiero. Te amo. Estoy locamente enamorado de ti.*''

"You don't! You aren't! Cal—''

But Cal had swept her into his embrace and was waltzing her around on the uneven slope, singing a bawdy Spanish bar song at the top of his lungs. A song that brought the faintest of smiles to even Sanches's lips. Then, coming to such a sudden halt under the apple tree that she was thrown against his chest, Cal addressed the fascinated students. "Flowers are one of the many ways to a woman's heart,'' he said. Breaking a branch from the tree, he bowed from the waist and presented it to Joanna with another wicked grin. "Do not scorn me, fairest of the fair, for I am sick with love.''

"You'll get fined for vandalism and it would take ten orchards of apple trees to make me spend even a minute of my time with you!''

"She's rejecting me," Cal said to Luis. "As we say here, she's playing hard to get…shut up, Joanna, you're interrupting the lesson. But do I accept defeat? No, I do not. Since candlelight, wine and a band of Gypsy violinists aren't immediately available, I'll have to improvise. *Improvisar.*'' He dropped to his knees in front of Joanna and clasped her hands. "'Come live with me and be my love,'" he intoned. "How's that for starters?" Then he further spoiled the effect by winking at her. "In fact, you can marry me if you like."

She hardened her heart against the laughter gleaming in his gray eyes. "I don't like."

Angelica said with a practiced pout, "Our teacher, she is *loca, muy loca*. A man such as this...one could wait forever for such a man."

Cal didn't even look around. "If you were to marry me, dearest Joanna, it would solve several of my problems. And yours too, I'd be willing to bet. I have a lot of money, *querida*. Quite an astonishing amount of money. Think of the fun you could have spending it."

As it happened, in the last few months Joanna had taken enormous pride in earning her own money and paying her own bills. No inheritance from her parents to smooth her path. No husband to reduce her to penury. Just what she herself was earning and choosing to spend. She glanced around and said sweetly, "What he means is that when flowers, candlelight and wine fail, a man waves his cash in front of a woman so that she'll succumb to his many charms. Of course, if he'd had any charms to start with, she'd already have succumbed."

"Oh, Joanna," Cal said, getting to his feet and brushing off the knees of his trousers, "how can you be so cruel?"

"It's easy, believe me."

"Then," said Cal to Luis, "as a last resort, there's always sex. *Sexo. Comprendes?*"

"Cal Freeman, I'll—"

But Cal had already enveloped her in his arms. Her last thought was how white his teeth were against his tanned skin. White and predatory. Then she stopped thinking altogether.

Ten seconds—or could it have been ten minutes?—later,

Cal released her. The small crowd of students clapped loudly, Luis producing a piercing wolf whistle. Joanna gaped at them with the air of a woman who had no idea where she was. Not even at the Winnipeg airport had Cal kissed her so comprehensively, with such single-minded passion and such total possessiveness.

She'd liked it. Who was she kidding? She'd adored it.

She'd succumbed.

Her shirt was rucked out of her waistband, and her hair had fallen loose of its pins to tumble down her back. How had that happened? Looking from Luis to Angelica to Sanches, she said fiercely, "Sex and liking are not always related. Let alone sex and love. Or sex and marriage. Remember that. And now we're walking over to the parking lot where we'll finish the lesson by talking about cars. Mr. Freeman will not be joining us."

Disdaining to tuck in her shirt or fix her hair, she put words into action. The students followed her, chattering to each other in Spanish. She should have prevented this; they were supposed to use only English during the lessons. But she didn't have the nerve to face them yet, let alone chide them. Besides, if she turned around, she might see that Cal was following them.

And if he was, what would she do? Scream at him like a shrew? Beg him for another of those glorious kisses? Oh, God, what was wrong with her?

How could she be filled with joy, rage and desire simultaneously?

How could she have responded to him when she hated the ground he walked on?

CHAPTER SIX

W<small>HEN</small> Joanna eventually reached the parking lot, she saw to her infinite relief that Cal was still standing under the apple tree. He hadn't followed them. He'd taken the hint. Quelling a pang she refused to call disappointment, she tried to gather her wits. The rest of the lesson wasn't as coherent as she might have wished; but it was a small miracle that she could put words together in one language, let alone two. Finally the clock on the bell tower struck four. With a bright smile she said, "That's all for today. See you Thursday afternoon, we'll meet in the classroom at two-thirty."

Angelica said with the utmost seriousness, "You give me this man's telephone number?"

"I threw it away," Joanna replied truthfully; at the Winnipeg airport she'd tossed the piece of paper Cal had given her into the nearest waste bin. "Anyway, the last I heard, he's got a woman and she sure isn't me."

"Que lástima."

"A pity, indeed," said Joanna, and watched her students wander off, talking animatedly among themselves. About her, she'd be willing to bet, and with no surprise turned around to find Cal striding toward her across the grass. No point in running or trying to hide. He'd only follow.

So she held her ground, her heart thudding in her chest. His play-acting under the apple tree had been all very amusing; but why was he really here? When he was close enough to hear her, Joanna said coldly, "You could have gotten me fired with that little exhibition. Is that what you want? Or do you even care?"

69

He'd thrust his hands in his pockets and was standing a careful distance away from her. "I haven't seen you for the better part of five months and I got carried away," he said. "I'm not going to apologize for that. But I do owe you an apology for something much more important. Ten days ago I was in Switzerland, where I visited my old friend Ludo Galliker—he's a guide who knew Gustave, and who met you at least twice. He straightened me out on a number of things. He told me Gustave was the one doing the cheating in your marriage. And spending all your money into the bargain. Joanna, I'm so sorry I believed Gustave's parents and Franz, rather than you. More sorry than I can say."

His voice was raw with sincerity, his gaze not faltering from hers. "Oh," she said blankly.

"I don't know what held me back from trusting you— although maybe, in a crazy way, it was your astonishing beauty. I was so bowled over by you, so off kilter, that my judgment was way off, too. Which is no excuse for the way I behaved, I know."

"I don't really—"

"I can't make reparation for what I did," Cal went on. "Can't ask you to forgive me. But I don't want to just vanish from your life, either. I'd like us to start over, as though January never happened. Because I can't get you out of my mind—and I'll be honest, I've tried. Tried very hard."

"Cal," she said deliberately, "what about your mistress in Boston?" And saw, to her great satisfaction, that for once she'd knocked him off balance.

"I don't have a mistress in Boston."

Her eyes narrowed. "Oh yes, you do—you talked to her on the phone at the Strassens', you called her *darling* and *sweetheart* and said you'd be together in the summer…I heard you. How dare you kiss me the way you did, and tell me you want to start over when there's another woman in your life?''

"The only person I talked to at the Strassens' was Lenny.''

"So who's Lenny? Another of your women?''

"Lenny's my daughter. My thirteen-year-old daughter.''

Joanna's jaw dropped. "Your *daughter?*''

"She goes to school in Switzerland. I try and phone her every couple of days. I'm a widower, Joanna...my wife died six years ago. I'm not involved with anyone, haven't been for some time.''

Joanna gaped at him, quite unable to think of anything to say; the odd thing was that she believed him immediately. And of all the emotions seething in her breast, sheer relief was uppermost. Relief that Cal hadn't been cheating on her. That he was free.

Free? she thought. Free for what?

Relief was instantly eclipsed by fear. She wasn't going to get involved with Cal Freeman. One charismatic mountaineer in her lifetime was enough for any woman. She couldn't afford to make a second mistake. The results were too painful, too all-encompassing. Too costly in all senses of the word.

So Gustave wasn't really in her past, she thought unhappily. She'd been fooling herself back in January to think she'd exorcised him merely by visiting his parents. The scars he'd left on her psyche were too deep to be so easily removed; maybe she'd carry them for the rest of her life.

She said with careful truth, "Thank you for coming all this way to apologize for not believing me, Cal. And for explaining about your daughter. It makes me feel better about you—that you weren't cheating on another woman when you kissed me. But that's it. I have nothing else to say to you. Anyway, I have to go now, I'm meeting a friend in a few minutes.''

As Cal took a step closer, she instinctively shrank back. He stopped dead in his tracks; he looked appalled. "Joanna, are you afraid of me?"

Afraid of what happened to her when he kissed her: yes. "I'm rebuilding my life. And it doesn't include you."

"But there's something between us—admit it."

"Sure—it's called *sexo*," she flashed. "Let me tell you this much—in the last four years, I made love with Gustave exactly once, which is when I got pregnant, and I haven't made love with anyone else. Surely I don't need to spell it out any clearer than that?"

"Dammit, it's more than deprivation!" Cal exploded. "In January I thought that's what I was suffering from, too. But ever since I met you, I haven't wanted to be within ten feet of another woman. I can't explain it. I only know it's true."

She hadn't wanted to be with the registrar, admirable man though he was. In fact, he'd bored her to distraction. She pushed this thought back down where it belonged. "I'm sure you'll get over it," she said.

"I'm not nearly as sure as you seem to be. Give us another chance—that's all I'm asking. At least let me take you out for dinner this evening."

With the sense that she was making one of those decisions that would affect the rest of her life, Joanna said tersely, "No. Thank you."

"*No?* Is that all you can say?"

"It's a perfectly good word. Even if you have difficulty understanding it."

"I have difficulty believing you can't see what's in front of your nose! Come on, Joanna, admit the truth. There's a huge attraction between us, and we'd be fools to turn our backs on it. And I refuse to call it nothing but lust." His smile was ironic. "Even though I've had more X-rated dreams in the last few months than in the rest of my life put together.''

Two nights ago, she'd been rolling around in an alpine meadow with Cal, as naked as the day she was born. A fiery blush mounted her cheeks. Cal said, his grin cracking his face, ''So I'm not the only one. Thank goodness for that.''

''It is lust,'' she said furiously. ''And even if it weren't, are you totally oblivious? Do you think I'd risk getting involved with another sexy mountain climber? I did that once, and it was a disaster. I'm not nineteen anymore, I'm twenty-eight—I've learned a thing or two. I'll never get involved with you. Never.''

''I am not Gustave Strassen,'' Cal said tightly.

''I'm happy here,'' she said wildly. ''I'm paying my own way, getting rid of my debts, making new friends and spending time with old ones. The last thing I need is a man in my life. And if you can't get that through your head, then you're not half as smart as I think you are.''

''Life moves on—that's something *I've* learned in the last few years. You can choose to go with it. Or you can close yourself off from it.''

''Keep your fancy philosophizing, I don't need it. Any more than I need you. The answer's no, Cal. No, no, no— why don't you get it?''

Then, from the corner of her eye, Joanna saw a tall blond woman emerge from the side door of the arts building. With huge relief she said, ''There's Sally, I've got to go. I don't want you in my life…it's that simple. Thank you for apologizing and goodbye.''

She wheeled and ran across the pavement, waving at Sally. Sally and Dianne were her two best friends; they'd been a trio at high school and now they were together again. Safe and undemanding friendships. She didn't need Cal. Who was neither safe nor undemanding.

"Hi, Sally," she called breathlessly. "Let's go to the S.U.B. and get a milkshake, I've had the day from hell."

"Who's the guy?" Sally asked. "Pretty darn cute."

"I'll tell you about him if you promise you won't ever mention his name again."

"Hmm," said Sally. "Maybe. Give, Joanna."

Without a backward look, Joanna headed for the Student Union Building. She was finished with Cal. Now that he'd apologized, she'd be able to forget him. Really forget him. She said rapidly, "When I was out west in January taking Gustave's personal effects to his parents, that man you just saw—well, I guess he saved my life. And now he's come back to haunt me."

Sally took her by the arm and steered her past the S.U.B. "This calls for a beer—we're going to the pub," she announced. "Why didn't you tell me and Dianne about this when you came back?"

"Because I wanted to forget about it. About him."

"Listen, I may have only gotten within forty feet of him, but that's one sexy dude."

"Sexy," Joanna said bitterly. "You can have him. He's all yours."

"From the look of him, he's not interested in anyone but you."

"He doesn't understand no. It's not a complicated word but he has a problem with it. A serious problem. Sally, I'll tell you what happened out west and you can pass it on to Dianne, and that's the end of it. *Hemos terminado.*"

"I'm meeting Dianne for supper at Tonio's Pizza, then we're going to the movies. Why don't you join us?"

And have the inquisition continue? "No, thanks, I'm going home, I've got a stack of papers to mark," Joanna said, pushing open the door to the student pub. Quickly she found a table and sat down facing her friend. "Now pay attention, because I'm only going through this once."

"You're being extremely belligerent," Sally said, her sky-blue eyes resting on her friend's flushed face. "That guy sure has gotten to you. Unlike Eugene."

Eugene was the registrar. "I'm not ready to date," Joanna said shortly. "It's too soon."

Sally signaled the waitress, ordered two chilled beers, and said, "Give, Joanna Strassen. And I want all the details."

"You're clean out of luck," said Joanna, and found she was blushing again. Fortunately it was dark. She fished in her wallet, paid for the beers, and began to talk. And all the while, as she spilled out the tale of that disastrous visit to the prairies, was achingly aware that she'd just sent Cal away. Definitively and definitely away.

He wouldn't be back. He was too proud a man for that.

This time, it really was goodbye.

His jaw clenched, Cal watched Joanna run across the pavement, her bare legs flashing in the sun, her sheaf of black hair skimming her back. Away from him. Away from him for good.

To her, he was just one more mountaineer. To be avoided at any cost. Like an avalanche. Or a crevasse deep as the one on the Western Cwm.

Time to go home, he thought. Go home and lick his wounds.

But where was home? The farm in Vermont, notable for Lenny's absence? His flat in Paris? His condo in New York? All equally luxurious and equally empty.

Lonely? Him? He was completely self-sufficient, had been for years.

No, she'd said. No. A short and unequivocal word.

He fumbled in his pocket for the keys of the red minivan, which he'd rented at the Halifax airport. He'd find a phone in town and make a reservation to fly back to New York tonight. There was an auction there the day after tomorrow of stringed instruments, including a rare Stradivari cello from the early seventeen hundreds. He should be there. He would be there.

No use staying here.

His gut felt hollow, and his hands were cold. What was wrong with him? So she'd said no. So what? She was just a woman, and it wasn't as though females weren't thick on the ground.

She was the only woman he'd ever met that he knew—knew in his bones—he had to take to bed if he was to have another moment's peace. The two of them naked, body and soul.

And explain that, Cal Freeman.

He couldn't. But it was true. Of course he'd wanted to bed Suzanne, he'd been young and in love. But he'd felt none of the desperation, the fierce compulsion, that drove him toward Joanna. None of the life-or-death intensity.

So was he going to turn tail and run, back to the Jasmines and Aleshas who until now had been enough for him?

When he'd told Joanna about his daughter, she'd been relieved. More than relieved, he'd swear to it. Up until then, she'd obviously assumed he was taken. Involved with a woman in Boston: and consequently unfaithful. Betraying another woman's trust. Like Gustave.

But now she knew better.

Today everything had all happened too fast. Too publicly. He'd been a fool to have kissed her under the apple tree, but she'd looked so beautiful, so familiar, so... essential. He raked his fingers through his hair. Damned if he was going to turn tail and run for the airport. He didn't want Alesha or Jasmine. He wanted Joanna. And he was going to do his level best to get her.

Plan B, he thought. Sit in his van and watch the main gates of the university, and pray that Joanna left for home that way. And if she didn't, then tomorrow he'd go to her office and he wouldn't leave until…until what, Cal? Until she called campus security and had him forcibly ejected?

If he could climb Everest, he could surely persuade one woman to have dinner with him.

For the next hour Cal sat in his van, drumming his fingers on the wheel, failing utterly to concentrate on a copy of the local paper he'd been given on the plane. The sun disappeared behind a tower of dark-edged cumulus; the sky darkened, suiting his mood exactly. Not once in his life had he waited for a woman like this. They'd always flocked to him, and over the years he'd come to take this for granted.

Was it only Joanna's beauty that had him by the throat? Or was it more? The stoicism he'd sensed in her, the dignity, the intelligence. Her loyalty to a husband who hadn't deserved it.

What had happened to the baby she was carrying?

She hadn't had an abortion; he'd swear to that.

Fifty-five minutes he'd been waiting, and it felt like forever. The wind had come up, petals whirling to the ground around the apple tree whose branch he'd broken off. And then he saw a woman in purple shorts come down the hill on a bicycle, concentrating on keeping her balance in the wind. She braked at the main gate, turned right and headed into town.

His heart pounding, Cal turned the key in the ignition and drove after her. All along the main street, he kept a couple of cars between his van and her bike. Thunder rolled in the distance, overriding the sound of the traffic. She pedaled past the last of the stores and neatly shingled houses of the town; farms replaced them, massed purple clouds casting a lurid light over the vibrant green of the hayfields. Head down against the wind, Joanna cycled another mile before turning down an unpaved lane edged with orchards of apple trees in full bloom.

With dramatic suddenness, lightning forked in the sky, bathing the blossoms in eerie blue-white. In a clap of thunder worthy of a horror film, the storm broke. Rain hit Cal's windshield with a rat-tat like bullets, pinged off the leaves, bounced in the dirt; a rain so heavy he had to slow down. He put on his turn signal and followed Joanna down the lane. No point in secrecy now. Pressing his palm on the horn, he drove past her, and pulled up at the edge of the ditch. Jumping out, he waved her down.

She slewed to a stop in the greasy mud, putting her sandal down in a puddle that he was quite sure she hadn't even noticed. Over the drumming rain and seethe of wind, she cried, "You follow me any further down this lane and I'll call the police!"

He grabbed her by the elbow, the feel of her slick, wet skin rocketing through his senses, and yelled back, "I'll put your bicycle in the van and drive you home."

She shook free. "I'm not afraid of a thunderstorm!"

The next bolt of lightning didn't even make her flinch. With a big grin Cal hollered, "You don't need to be afraid of me, either."

"I'm more afraid of drowning in this puddle than I am of you."

"Fine," Cal said, and took the bike by the handlebars. "The passenger door's unlocked."

"I'm not going anywhere with you!"

Her hair was wrapped around her throat in soaked black strands; he said with all the intensity he was capable of, "I'm the one in danger of drowning. In your eyes, in your beauty and defiance and courage."

She swallowed hard. "I—"

"If you don't want me to touch you, or kiss you, I won't. I swear I won't."

"That's not—"

"Not what, Joanna?" he said with sudden gentleness,

for weren't her eyes blurred with something other than rain?

"You do scare me," she blurted.

"I don't mean to."

A rainsquall lashed at her cheeks. Staring straight at him, she quavered, "You don't just scare me—you terrify me. I thought Gustave was part of my past. But he isn't. I can't afford to get hurt again, Cal, I just can't, don't you *see?*"

She was being as honest as she could be, he thought, and fought down the impulse to take her in his arms, hold her tight to his chest and never let her go. "I don't want to hurt you or frighten you," he said hoarsely.

Her eyes dropped. "It's all too soon," she whispered.

Thunder rattled the sky like a band of percussionists. Raising his voice, he said, "At least let me drive you home. You're soaked."

With the faintest of smiles she said, "So are you."

Rain was trickling down the back of his neck, plastering his shirt to his chest. He grinned at her. "Get in. I'll throw your bike in the back."

For a long moment she stood still. Cal held his breath, hoping she couldn't see the banging of his heart under his wet shirt. Then she relinquished her hold on the bike, turned and climbed into the red minivan. Cal let out his pent-up breath in a long sigh. So far, so good. The next step of Plan B was to convince her to have dinner with him.

After he'd put the bike in the van, he, too, climbed in, favoring his left knee, the one he'd injured three years ago in a fall on the south ridge of Kongur. It always bothered him in wet weather. Joanna's hand was resting on the door handle; she looked very much like a woman about to change her mind. He said calmly, "How far do I have to go?"

She bit her lip. "Half a mile. It's a white-painted cottage on the right."

Cal eased his foot onto the accelerator and concentrated on his driving, for the van seemed to be intent on finding every pothole and mud slick on the road. As he went around the last corner, the rain lessened as dramatically as it had started. The road opened into a field beyond which was a magnificent panorama of the bay and the far red cliffs. On the expanse of open water, the waves curvetted like white-maned stallions. As lightning split the sky, he said inadequately, "That's quite the view."

"I'm very lucky to have found this place...the owners are on sabbatical for eight months."

The cottage, white-shingled, was surrounded by a tall hedge of old-fashioned lilacs; it had a front porch, a field-stone chimney and a small vegetable patch. It was like a miniature version of his property in Vermont, Cal thought with a quickening of his pulse. Joanna would like "Riversedge." Not for her the safe little bungalow in town. He said, "I'll get your bike."

"Thanks," she said with notable brevity.

He wheeled the bike to the front of the cottage, trying to disguise his limp, and hefted it onto the porch. Then he said without emphasis, "May I come in?"

She was facing him in the open front door, her eyes as dark as the massed thunderclouds. "You're awfully wet," she said reluctantly. "But I don't—"

"I've got dry clothes in my suitcase in the van. At least let me change before I drive to the airport."

She frowned at him. "Well, all right. But—"

As another rainsquall whipped across the bay toward the cottage, Cal headed for the van. He grabbed his bag, climbed the porch stairs and pulled the screen door open, stepping inside. Joanna was standing only four feet from the door, her gaze far from friendly. "The bathroom's over there," she said.

"You go first, you're wetter." He grinned. "And muddier."

As she glanced down at her bare legs, which were liberally splashed with red clay, he added solemnly, "Did you ever think of a career in modelling?"

"Not skinny enough and I'm too old."

"Your body's perfect and you're just the right age," Cal said huskily.

She gave a hunted look around the small room and said breathlessly, "I won't be long."

"Put on a dress," he said deliberately, "we'll go to that inn that overlooks the bay. The one with the fabulous scallops and the famous raspberry flan."

"I can't afford even one scallop in that place, let alone a plateful!"

"I'm paying. Part of the apology."

"One thing about you, you're persistent."

"You're worth being persistent for. Lousy grammar, but you get my drift."

"Dinner," Joanna said with an edge of desperation. "Just dinner."

"That's all I'm offering," he countered, a gleam in his eye. "Take your time, Joanna, I'll make a reservation for an hour from now."

She glanced at his soaked knit shirt. "They have a dress code, you have to have a proper shirt and tie."

"Don't you worry, I won't disgrace you."

She made a rude noise, turned on her heel and scurried into her bedroom, emerging a few minutes later with clothes over her arm. Then she vanished into the bathroom.

Cal twisted his shoulders to rid them of tension. His shirt was clammy against his skin, the rain was drumming on the roof, and he felt wonderful. He checked the number in his wallet, picked up the phone and made a reservation at the inn; then he went out to the van and brought in his luggage. Finally, he looked around the room with frank curiosity.

Simple furnishings, colorful braided rugs, a stone fireplace, and in the far corner a desk with a computer. He wandered over to it, remembering how single-mindedly Joanna had concentrated on her laptop in the back bedroom at the Strassens'. A neat pile of galley proofs sat by the computer, a title page on the top. "*A Time for Wild Swans,* by Ann Cartwright," he read.

Cal stood still, his brain racing. Ann Cartwright's first novel had come out two years ago, to much critical acclaim; he'd read it en route to an auction in Tuscany, and found its combination of poetic intensity and stark emotion very moving. So was Joanna Strassen the author of that novel?

The words at the bottom of the title page leaped out at him. Copyright: Joanna Strassen.

His intuition, that had refused to allow him to forget her, had been dead-on. Her intelligence, her anguish and fiery temper, her complexity, he'd known them already from her book.

She was as different from Suzanne as a woman could be. And she'd agreed—if with no enthusiasm whatsoever—to have dinner with him.

Then his mind made another leap: one by one the thoughts clicked through his brain. Lenny loved poetry and adored reading novels. Lenny needed a mother, as Ludo had so cogently pointed out. Who better than Joanna?

Add to that the fact that Joanna was presumably teaching at the university to keep her head above water: critically acclaimed first novels didn't often translate into money in the bank. Besides, she'd mentioned debts, undoubtedly Gustave's. So Joanna needed money. He, Cal, had money. More than enough for both of them. He could marry her.

Solve all his problems with Lenny, and give Joanna the time to write without having to worry about paying the rent.

He could take her to bed.

Isn't that what he'd wanted since the first moment he'd gazed into her unconscious face on the snowswept prairie?

Adrenaline surging through his veins, Cal strode over to the window, staring unseeingly at the wet, windswept orchard. Joanna as his wife. Yes, he thought. Yes.

CHAPTER SEVEN

JOANNA twisted around to make sure the label wasn't showing on her dress. She felt as uncertain and shy as if this were her first date. I'm a twenty-eight-year-old widow, she thought. Cal Freeman is just a man, and we're only going out for dinner. I'm not marrying him, for heaven's sake.

I'm not marrying anyone. Ever again.

Somewhat heartened, she decided her deep red lipstick looked fine with the dress, an indigo calf-length shift slit to the knee; what she didn't see was how the simplicity of the dress artfully called attention to her figure, to the coil of silken hair at her nape, to the elegant line of her brows and the haunting shadows under her cheekbones. She was, instead, rather pleased that her eyeshadow and mascara had gone on so smoothly, considering that her fingers had felt all thumbs. She slipped on her sandals, inserted antique silver earrings from Tibet into her lobes, and gathered up her small evening purse.

There. She was ready.

Time to face Cal.

She walked out into the living room and said coolly, "I've put towels on the shelf. I hope I haven't been too long?"

He'd been staring out the window. He turned around, and she saw with a jangling of her nerves the utter stillness that seized his tall frame. Only his eyes moved, flickering up and down her body.

With a huge effort Joanna kept silent, forcing herself to breathe through the tightness in her chest. Finally Cal said, a note in his voice new to her, "Joanna, I—you're so utterly beautiful, I don't know what to say. Only that I'll be the most fortunate man in the whole dining room. Hell, the most fortunate man in the province.'' His smile was crooked. ''How about the continent, the world and the universe?''

Tears pricked at her lids. Gustave had always denigrated her beauty, perhaps hoping to subjugate her that way. ''Thank you,'' she mumbled. ''I hope you're not cold, waiting in your wet clothes.''

''I'm fine. Five minutes.''

He picked up his bag and walked past her into the bathroom. Slowly she let out her breath. She was playing a dangerous game, she knew that. Because hadn't part of her hoped Cal would take her in his arms and kiss her as he'd kissed her in the orchard a few hours ago?

Hoped? Craved would be a more accurate word, she thought crazily. The mere thought of kissing Cal spread an ache of desire through her body. Desire such as she hadn't felt for years. If ever.

She couldn't give in to it. Couldn't, wouldn't, mustn't.

Focus on the scallops, she told herself. Scallops, raspberries and small talk. That's all she had to do. Surely she could manage that.

To her ears came the buzz of Cal's razor. A small, intimate sound, that made nonsense of her resolutions. As did their table at the inn half an hour later, a table set apart from the others, overlooking the water and softly bathed in candlelight. And then there was Cal. His lightweight suit fit him to perfection, subtly emphasizing the strength of his shoulders, his lean belly and long legs; while his silk shirt and tie breathed money and the power that money conveys.

But Cal's power came from within, Joanna thought unwillingly. Nothing to do with his clothes or his money, and everything to do with a confidence and masculinity that were bone-deep. ''Something to drink?'' he said.

"I'll have wine with the meal," she replied, adding unwisely, "I need my head clear when I'm with you."

"That's encouraging," he said dryly.

Quickly they dealt with the menu and the choice of wine. The waiter brought delicious crunchy rolls, hot from the oven. Going on the attack, Joanna said, "I noticed you're limping."

"A fall in a slide on the Kongur massif. It only bothers me in damp weather."

She said with hostile emphasis, "I long ago decided that all mountaineers have a death wish."

His jaw tightened. "You can count me out on that one."

"Then why do you risk your life time and again?"

So she wanted warfare, did she? "For glory, of course," he said fliply.

Her nostrils flared. "It's a real question, Cal."

He put down his knife. "For a whole lot of reasons. Pushing myself to my limits, and beyond. Trying to align myself with the mountain, so that we're allies, not opponents. Craving the elemental beauty of snow, ice, sky and rock, and the utter silence of the peak. Where you're always alone, no matter who's with you." He ran his fingers through his hair. "That'll do for a start."

And those accomplishments, she thought with an inward shiver, were surely a major source of his power. She said sharply, "You didn't mean to tell me all that."

"I never talk about that stuff. I just do it."

"Not even to your daughter? To Lenny?"

"Lenny's never asked…I don't really know how she feels about me climbing." He gave an exasperated sigh. "Which is something else I've never told anyone."

All Joanna's resolutions to keep her distance flew through the window. "Why me?"

He said obliquely, "I saw your manuscript on the desk. I know you're Ann Cartwright."

"Darn it," she muttered, "I'd forgotten about the proofs." Then her eyes widened. "You think I'm pumping you," she said, horrified, "so that I can use you in a book?"

"No, Joanna, I don't mean that at all. I read your first book, I know you're capable of understanding what I'm getting at with the mountains."

Briefly she closed her eyes. "Gustave climbed for glory. He was always trying to beat the other guy, to conquer and be lionized."

"And you didn't intend to tell me that."

Her smile was twisted. "The plan was to keep you at arm's length emotionally and physically," she said glibly.

He leaned forward, his eyes like gimlets. "Neither one is possible with you and me."

She dragged her gaze away, and to her infinite relief saw the waiter approach with the wine. Once he'd left, Cal raised his glass. "To us," he said.

"To me and to you," she flashed.

"Two separate entities, is that what you mean?"

"Precisely."

"But I refuse to accept that."

"You may not have any choice."

"I've read your book—it was a fine book, by the way, full of nuance and hard-earned wisdom. So I know you're a risk-taker. You were pushing your limits with that book just as I push mine on the ridges and ice fields."

She took a long drink of her wine, savoring its aftertaste. "It's one thing to push limits at the computer. Another to push them in bed. Because that's what we're talking about."

He laughed, his teeth very white. "I like you," he said spontaneously. "You say it like it is. Sexual attraction is most certainly a big part of what's going on."

"The answer's no," she said very quietly.

"Did Gustave damage you that much?" he asked, equally quietly.

She raised her chin. "Yes, he did."

For a moment Cal's features were suffused with an anger all the more powerful for being contained. "Bastard," he said.

"Not really," she responded wryly. "After all, you met his parents."

"Yeah…" His smile was wry. "Odds are they're legally married, wouldn't you say?"

"Definitely." As the waiter brought their salads, she deftly changed the subject. "Tell me about your daughter."

"Lenny? Thirteen years old, acts nine some days and twenty others. Skis competitively, writes poetry, reads voraciously, takes in every stray animal in miles, one day she wants to be a vet, the next day she's going to be president and run the country right…" He smiled ruefully. "Don't get me started."

"What grade is she in?"

"She's going to school in Switzerland this year."

"Oh? Why?"

"I'm often away, with my job or on an expedition. I felt it was better for her to be in an all girls' school with female teachers." He moved his shoulders restlessly. "But she doesn't like being away from home—we live by a river in Vermont."

"How could you send her away?" Joanna demanded, glaring at him. To have a child and then send her thousands of miles across the ocean to go to school? What kind of a father was he?

"I thought it was for the best. And, of course, the skiing there is out of this world."

"There's more to life than mountains, Cal. Why don't you get married and provide her with a mother and a proper home?"

So Joanna was the one to bring the subject up. His nerves tightened. "I should get married, I know I should."

Discovering she didn't want to picture an unknown woman living with Cal, sharing his bed and his life, Joanna snapped, "Why don't you? I'm sure you must meet lots of women."

"Never found the right one."

His flippancy infuriated her. Patches of pink staining her cheekbones, she retorted, "If I had a daughter, I'd want her with me. Especially at thirteen, that's such a vulnerable age."

"Joanna, what happened to the baby?"

The color drained from her cheeks. Her lashes flew down to hide her eyes, her fingers tightening around the stem of her glass. Cal said abruptly, "I'm sorry, I shouldn't have asked."

His question had come out of the blue. Yet wasn't her vehemence about Lenny's exile a direct result of her own experiences? And didn't she, deep down, want Cal to think well of her? To know the truth about the loss of her child? Joanna said rapidly, her voice purged of emotion, "Gustave came to visit me last July. I hadn't seen him for a couple of years—ever since the money ran out. He was full of contrition. He'd had a near escape on those rock towers in Patagonia and it had changed him, he said. He swore he'd be a better husband, that he'd be faithful to me, and that he loved me."

Absently she twirled the glass on the linen tablecloth, her thoughts a long way away. "I no longer loved him. I hadn't for months...there'd been too many betrayals. But this time he was so sincere, so sorry for the way he'd behaved in the past that I felt I had to try again—I took my marriage vows very seriously, you see. I know that's old-fashioned, but that's the way it was."

She glanced up. Cal's eyes were trained on her face, his

big body very still. "We went to bed together," she said flatly. "I completely forgot I hadn't been using birth control pills, what was the point of using them, Gustave hadn't been home for ages—so I got pregnant." She stared fixedly into the pale gold wine, shot through with candlelight. "As it turned out, Gustave's visit had nothing to do with contrition. My great-aunt Lucy had died and left me some money...he stayed around long enough to get his hands on it and then he took off. To organize the Annapurna expedition, so I found out later."

"Joanna..."

Cal rested his lean fingers on her hand, stilling its restless movements. She stared down at the narrow ridge of scars on his knuckles, feeling the warmth of his skin seep into hers. "I was three months pregnant when Gustave radioed me from the second base camp on Annapurna, it was the first time I'd talked to him since his visit. He needed more money, that was the reason for getting in touch...but I didn't have any to give him. Anyway, I told him about the baby." Keeping her words steady with an effort, she went on, "The very next day Gustave was killed in a fall. Franz, of course, blamed me totally."

"And then?"

"I was in our Toronto condo when I got the message, dressing to go out and do a couple of errands before I settled down to write. For some reason I decided after the phone call that I should still do the errands. So I set off anyway. There'd been a heavy frost that night. Crossing the park, I slipped and fell." In a ragged voice, she finished, "Because of the fall, I lost the baby...I should never have gone out, I don't know why I did, it was such a stupid thing to do."

"You were in shock, Joanna. Not thinking straight."

She couldn't bear the compassion in his voice. "I should have stayed home!"

He stated the obvious. "So you blame yourself."

She nodded miserably, tapping her fingernails against the heavy crystal. "Wouldn't you?"

"You did the best you could. For years you did your best. What more can any of us do?"

"I suppose so," she mumbled. "I'm sorry, Cal, I didn't mean to dump all this on you."

"You're not dumping, you're sharing some hard truths with me...which in a way is quite a compliment."

She gave him a faint smile. "Well, that's one way of looking at it."

"I'm sorry you lost the baby," he said gently.

Only Sally and Dianne knew how much she'd longed for that baby, despite the fact that she no longer loved the man who'd conceived it; and how cruel a blow her loss had been. She pulled her hand free, saying with attempted lightness, "It's over and done with, isn't it? Here comes the waiter. It might be ten years before I eat here again, I'm determined to enjoy every bite."

Cal sat back. So the confidences were over, he thought; and knew that in a very short time he'd learned a lot about Joanna, about her vulnerabilities and her strengths. The only unpalatable fact—apart from the fact that he couldn't wipe the floor with Gustave Strassen—was that she in no way had connected Cal's need for a wife with herself.

So what was the next step in his plan? Charm her, he decided. Relax her so that she let down her guard. He topped up her wineglass and lifted his salad fork. "Did you do much traveling with Gustave?"

"In the early years, yes," she said, and went on to describe some of her experiences in Tibet and southern Switzerland. From there they moved to Cal's job, then on to movies and politics. The candle was replaced with a fresh one. Joanna's unabashed enjoyment of the scallops and then of an Amaretto chocolate mousse touched Cal;

most of his dates took these small luxuries for granted. But Joanna, from the things she'd let drop, was living on the edge of poverty and had been for some time. That'll change, he vowed, and as their coffee was poured decided the moment was right to raise Plan C.

He said casually, "How long since you've had a vacation?"

Joanna laughed. "Vacation? What's that?"

"I have a proposal. Hear me out before you say anything."

Her smile had faded and she was looking at him warily. There was a small smudge of chocolate on her lip; Cal reached over, smoothing it away, and saw her eyes darken and her mouth tremble. "In a couple of weeks," he said, "I'm bringing Lenny back home to Vermont for the summer holidays. I'd like to treat you to a few days in Switzerland. You can fly over, I'll meet you in Zurich, and we'll drive to my chalet in Appenzell and then get Lenny. She'd like you, I know she would. And not just because you're a famous novelist."

"Hardly famous," Joanna said, her head whirling. Once again Cal had knocked her off balance. That streak of fire on her lip, and then an invitation that could mean only one thing. An affair. In which he'd foot the bill. "I can't do that," she muttered.

"Why not? You told me earlier you'll soon be finished with this group of students. So it's an ideal time for you to take a break."

"Cal, I don't have any money," she said with barely controlled impatience. "The royalties on my first book and the proceeds from the sale of the condo went to pay off some of my debts. My salary's a pittance. I'd scarcely be able to buy an ice cream in Switzerland, and I certainly won't accept money from you."

"I don't see why not."

"Just because you're rich, you can't buy me!"

He said evenly, "You'd sleep in the guest room, Joanna."

"You're all heart," she snapped. Perhaps she'd misjudged him about the affair. But what matter if she had? He had only to kiss her, and she'd climb into his bed quicker than you could say traveler's check. And that was the real reason she couldn't go anywhere near Switzerland.

"I'm asking a favor of you, that's all," Cal persisted. "I'd like you to meet Lenny, give me some advice. There are times she scares me half to death—I don't have a clue how to handle a teenage girl."

"And you think I have?"

"At least you've been one," he said with that crooked smile that always made her want to smile back.

"I can't go," she said with utter finality. "It's out of the question."

His eyes hardened. "Come on, Joanna, do I have to spell it out? It's payback time. I saved your life in January and now I'm asking a favor in return."

Her chin snapped up. "So you're a businessman to the core! Cost and benefit. That's a pretty crude way to treat another human being."

"It's not as though a trip to Switzerland would be any hardship," he said curtly.

For a treacherous moment Joanna allowed herself to imagine the alpine meadows, the astonishing physicality of the peaks, the tolling of cow bells and the flowers that tumbled from the window boxes. She desperately needed a holiday; and she'd always loved Switzerland, even in the worst of times with Gustave. Besides, she'd never been to the northeast; she and Gustave had always used Geneva as their home base, not Zurich. "I'm not going," she repeated, and drained her coffee cup.

"That I saved your life means nothing to you?"

"What do you want, a medal?"

"I want you to meet Lenny, tell me if you think she should stay in Switzerland next year or come home. That's all."

He wasn't going to give up. Gripping the edge of the table, Joanna said, "Let's be honest, Cal. You've kissed me, you know what happens when you do. Even if you promised me you wouldn't as much as touch me the whole time I was with you, I wouldn't trust that promise. So that's one more reason I won't go to Switzerland."

In a biting voice he said, "First, you're equating me with your husband, which is something I thoroughly dislike. Second, you're not being entirely truthful. It's yourself you don't trust. You want me just as much as I want you and don't bother denying it—I've held you in my arms, I know what I'm talking about."

His accuracy only made her angrier. "I'm not going!" she announced. "How many times do I have to say that? Drop it, it won't fly."

"We'll drop it for now. But I'm not through."

"*No* is a word you sure have trouble with."

"Whereas you have trouble with *yes*. You're afraid of coming to life again, that's your problem. I wouldn't have thought you were a coward—but I guess I'm wrong."

So angry she could scarcely speak, Joanna flared, "I was married to a man who deceived me financially and sexually for years, and who persisted in risking his life and the lives of others so he could get to the top of any peak that attracted his fancy. And now you're recommending I get involved with another mountain climber—namely you? Give me a break."

"Stop labeling me! I'm a hell of a lot more than someone who just climbs mountains."

Suddenly exhausted, Joanna said, "Cal, I don't want to fight with you like this. You did save my life and I'm so grateful to you. But that doesn't mean I'll do whatever you ask.''

Cal shoved his credit card in the folder with the bill and signaled to the waiter. "Let's get out of here."

They sat in silence until the bill was returned. Then Joanna said with deadly politeness, "Until you broached your crazy idea about Switzerland, I enjoyed myself very much. Thank you."

"I'll take you home."

"You're being a sore loser!"

"Oh, I haven't lost yet," he said softly, and gestured for her to precede him out of the dining room.

Joanna sat in a stony silence all the way back to her cottage. Cal pulled up as near to the front walk as he could; before she could unlatch her door, he slid to the ground and was striding around to open it for her. She climbed down, horribly aware of how close he was standing, the bulk of his body obscuring the garden behind him. She stepped back a pace, felt the heel of her sandal sink into the damp earth, and said frostily, "Good night."

And then he did what all evening had been inevitable: he took her in his arms, fastened his mouth on hers and kissed her as though she were the woman he'd been waiting for all his life. Kissed her with such raw hunger that she surrendered without a murmur. More than surrendered, she thought dimly: and knew she was meeting him on his own terms, hunger for hunger, demand with demand.

Her arms were around his neck, holding him so tightly that her breasts were strained to his chest. The heated thrust of his tongue made her moan with pleasure; like a reed to the wind she was pliant in his embrace. His hands were clasping her waist, smoothing her hips, pulling her so close that his arousal inflamed her, made her ache and throb with desire.

She'd never wanted Gustave so instantly, so fiercely. Her

whole body was on fire for Cal, desperate to be possessed by him; she whimpered his name, felt his lips slide down her throat and bury themselves in the hollow where her pulse was frantically racing. Then with one hand he cupped the soft weight of her breast, kneading it with exquisite gentleness. As her nipple hardened to his touch, she heard him mutter, "Joanna, you're so beautiful, I want you so much."

She raised his face to hers, so he could see the desire naked in her eyes, and for a long moment in the blossom-scented darkness of the lane they gazed at each other, a gaze every bit as intimate as his caresses. Then Cal leaned forward, letting his lips wander from her forehead to her eyelids, across her cheekbones to her mouth again, a trail of delicious sensation that made Joanna tremble like a leaf to the breeze.

As his kiss deepened, she abandoned herself to it, her hands drifting from his nape to his waist, searching out the long indentation of his spine, the taut muscles over his ribs, then, daringly, the hard jut of his hipbones. He rubbed himself against her until she was enveloped in nothing but need. Then he said hoarsely, his breath warm on her cheek, "Let's go inside…I want to make love to you."

Wasn't that what she wanted, too? Hadn't she discovered in Cal's arms in the last few minutes a woman she hardly recognized, passionate, wanton and hungry? She opened her mouth to say yes, and saw behind his head the solid outline of her little cottage, which had brought her such solace in the last few months. Her home. Her refuge. Her place of safety.

She was going to risk all that for a tumble in bed with a man she scarcely knew? A man used to women falling into his arms? In a voice she wouldn't have recognized as her own, she said, "We can't! We're not in love, we can't

GET FREE BOOKS and a FREE GIFT WHEN YOU PLAY THE...

777

Lucky 7

Just scratch off the silver box with a coin. Then check below to see the gifts you get!

SLOT MACHINE GAME!

YES! I have scratched off the silver box. Please send me the 2 free Harlequin Presents® books and gift for which I qualify. I understand I am under no obligation to purchase any books, as explained on the back of this card.

306 HDL DRRK   **106 HDL DRRZ**

FIRST NAME   LAST NAME

ADDRESS

APT.#   CITY

STATE/PROV.   ZIP/POSTAL CODE

7	7	7	**Worth TWO FREE BOOKS plus a BONUS Mystery Gift!**
🍒	🍒	🍒	**Worth TWO FREE BOOKS!**
♣	♣	♣	**Worth ONE FREE BOOK!**
🔔	🔔	🍒	**TRY AGAIN!**

Visit us online at www.eHarlequin.com

(H-P-01/03)

The Harlequin Reader Service® — Here's how it works:

Accepting your 2 free books and gift places you under no obligation to buy anything. You may keep the books and gift and return the shipping statement marked "cancel." If you do not cancel, about a month later we'll send you 6 additional books and bill you just $3.57 each in the U.S., or $4.24 each in Canada, plus 25¢ shipping & handling per book and applicable taxes if any.* That's the complete price and — compared to cover prices of $4.25 each in the U.S. and $4.99 each in Canada — it's quite a bargain! You may cancel at any time, but if you choose to continue, every month we'll send you 6 more books, which you may either purchase at the discount price or return to us and cancel your subscription.
*Terms and prices subject to change without notice. Sales tax applicable in N.Y. Canadian residents will be charged applicable provincial taxes and GST. Credit or debit balances in a customer's account(s) may be offset by any other outstanding balance owed by or to the customer.

just fall into bed because of—of lust. Because that's what it is. Nothing to do with feelings. Or real connection.''

''Maybe this is how we find the connection,'' he said huskily, nibbling at her lips with exquisite persuasiveness.

''And maybe it isn't—what then?'' In sudden despair she pushed herself away from him. ''This is exactly what I did when I was nineteen—fell into Gustave's arms. And paid for it for the next nine years.''

''How about this scenario? You fall into my arms and we find out it was the right thing to do?''

''And then you leave for Everest or Annapurna and I stay here worried sick about you? No, Cal, I've done that all too often, and I hated it.''

''What if I quit the mountains?''

''What are you saying? Quit something that's so important to you?'' She stepped back, staring into his shadowed features with strained intensity. ''You're surely not in love with me?''

''No,'' he said levelly, ''I'm not.''

So the scene in the orchard had been nothing but play-acting. Just as she'd suspected. ''If you quit the mountains, you'd resent me, I know you would. Maybe in a different lifetime something would have worked out between us. But in this lifetime, there's just too much against it. And I'm not into casual affairs, I never have been.'' She smoothed her dress down, her heartbeat still racketing in her chest. ''Look, it's late and I have to teach tomorrow morning. Thank you for dinner, and good luck with Lenny. Drive carefully, won't you?''

He said without inflection, ''I'll call you in a week about Switzerland. Think about it, Joanna. Are you going to live in Gustave's shadow for the rest of your life?''

''It's not that simple!''

''I think it is.'' He gave her an abrupt nod, turned on his heel and strode to the far side of the van. He was limping very slightly, she noticed with the only part of her brain that seemed to be working. Limping from an injury on the mountains.

Swiftly he reversed, and without a backward look drove away up the lane, the sound of the engine gradually diminishing until silence claimed the night again.

Joanna stood still. A week wouldn't make any difference. She wasn't going anywhere with Cal Freeman; and the sooner he accepted that, the better.

She wasn't a coward. She was just being sensible. Adult. Responsible. All the things she hadn't been at nineteen.

CHAPTER EIGHT

FOUR days later, Joanna parked her bicycle outside Sally's bungalow. Geraniums and lobelia lined the walk with pink, red and blue; orange California poppies and huge purple and yellow irises flanked the front door. Sally opened the door. "Hi, Joanna, Dianne's already here. We're out back on the patio. Like my garden?"

"It's very cheerful."

"I did get a little carried away. I'm sort of hoping the Liatris won't bloom until the poppies are done."

Liatris was magenta. "Hey, it's all nature," said Joanna. "I brought a bottle of wine."

"Great, thanks. The barbecue's on."

Sally's bungalow was as untidy as her garden was colorful. She coached basketball at the university and was steadfastly in love with a man called Albert who lived with his mother. As they emerged into the sunshine on the patio, Joanna blinked against the light. "Hi, Dianne."

Dianne was short, plump, and indolent, married to Peter, a marine biologist who was out at sea most of the summer. She waved her wineglass at Joanna. "You look gorgeous as usual," she said, without a speck of envy. Then her gaze sharpened. "Although do I detect circles under your eyes? What's up? The students getting to you?"

Joanna hadn't been sleeping well ever since Cal had left. "You know how it is," she said lightly. "They've suddenly realized our time's nearly up and they want to cram the entire English language into the last three lessons."

Dianne taught French at summer school. "I understand totally," she said, and proceeded to tell a very funny story

99

about a champion football player who'd flunked French twice already. In the meantime Sally grilled chicken and produced a Caesar salad from the refrigerator, which they followed up with one of Dianne's luscious, calorie-loaded desserts. Joanna sat back with a sigh. "Butterscotch cream pie, food for the gods. Good thing I'm biking home... Dianne, I forgot to ask how your sister is? You mentioned last week she might be having some tests."

Dianne's face clouded. "She got the results yesterday. She has thyroid cancer, they're going to operate next week."

"Cancer? How serious is it?"

Dianne's smile was wobbly. "Well, if you've got to get the big C, this is the kind to have. Slow-growing and easily contained. She'll have radiation afterward."

"You should have told us sooner," Sally said, distressed. "Here we were going on about Albert's mother and the perils of buying plants that don't turn out the right color...I'm so sorry she's sick."

"I planned to tell you, I just didn't want to put a damper on the meal. And I talked to Peter last night, he'll be home next week when Sara's scheduled for surgery. So that's good."

"You just never know, do you?" Joanna said, grimacing. "You chug along day to day doing all the stuff that has to be done, and then something like this happens."

"It does make you think," Dianne agreed. "Sara's always been so healthy, I guess I took that for granted."

They talked back and forth, getting more details of the treatment. Sally said finally, "*Carpe diem* isn't such a bad idea, is it? You know, I really wonder sometimes if I shouldn't break my engagement to Albert. When he told his mother he and I were going to spend a week at the beach in July, she promptly had an asthma attack. Now there's a woman who's as tough as a carthorse, she'll probably outlive me."

Dianne laughed. "You could try. Breaking it, I mean. Maybe it would shake him up."

"He can be so sweet," Sally said in exasperation. "Men! Why is it we can't live with them or without them? By the way, Joanna, what happened with that gorgeous hunk called Cal?"

"Sally told me about him," Dianne chimed in.

"Nothing," Joanna said.

Sally gave a rude snort. "Come clean."

Over the years the three had exchanged many confidences, and had never had a trust betrayed. Confident that they would share her views, Joanna said easily, "We had dinner together. He wants me to spend some time in Switzerland with him. Ostensibly to meet his daughter, who goes to school there. But really for a quickie affair."

"When are you leaving?" Dianne asked.

Joanna raised her brows. "I'm not. I said no."

"You *what?*" Sally squeaked.

"But why?" Dianne demanded.

"I'm not going to take off into the wild blue yonder with a man I don't know from Adam!"

"I saw him," Sally said. "His kind are rare on the ground. Especially in Harcourt."

"He saved your life," Dianne said. "You owe him."

"You'd be crazy to turn him down."

"Out of your mind."

"Anyway, you really need a holiday."

"We'll lend you some money so you can go."

"Sure we will, great idea, Di."

Joanna covered her ears. "Stop it, you two! I'm not going!"

"We think you should," Sally said firmly. "You should listen to us."

"You don't love Gustave anymore," Dianne put in. "So that's not an issue."

"But Cal's another mountaineer," Joanna protested.

"Come off it, Jo, you can keep him away from a few mountains," Sally said. "I mean, look at you, you're drop-dead gorgeous—and the man definitely had eyes in his head."

"But—"

"Time you broke loose, Joanna," Dianne announced. "Sally and I have been worried about you, wondering how you'd ever meet anyone in Harcourt. If even half of what Sally told me is true, this is quite a guy. Go for it."

Abruptly Sally sobered. "You know, there's another issue here. Even if you don't want to marry again, you do want a baby. We've always known that, ever since high school."

Joanna gaped at her. It was true. She'd wanted to have children for as long as she could remember.

"So here's your chance," Sally went on. "Go to Switzerland, get pregnant and come home."

"We'll knit you booties," said Dianne. "Pink ones and blue ones."

"*You'll* knit her booties," Sally said. "I'll buy her those cute little sleepers that babies seem to need. Green and yellow," she finished thoughtfully.

"Stop!" Joanna said wildly, grabbing her scalp with both hands. "You must be drunk, both of you—I can't go off to Switzerland to make a baby!"

"Stone-cold sober and of course you can," Sally said.

"And have a bit of fun in the process," Dianne added naughtily. As Joanna blushed scarlet, she added, "So you're not immune to him. Thank heavens, there's hope for you."

Remembering that impassioned embrace outside her cottage, Joanna wailed, "He just has to look at me and I melt. *Me*. Who's not into affairs."

"I'll drive you to the airport," Sally said.

"And we meant what we said about the money," Dianne seconded.

Joanna's throat tightened. "That's so sweet of you. Both of you. But I—"

"You can't go asking him for money every time you want to buy chocolate," Dianne said. "They make the best chocolate in the world in Switzerland."

"You could bring us back some," Sally teased.

"If I go," Joanna said weakly.

"When you go," her two friends chorused.

"But I've never had an affair in my life," Joanna blurted, "I wouldn't know how to behave."

Dianne rolled her eyes. "Just let nature take her course. Although there's no harm in taking a sexy nightgown to help her along."

With a quick glance at Joanna's flushed cheeks, Sally said, "How about you both help me load the dishwasher?"

Joanna surged to her feet and started gathering plates. What was she thinking of, even to hint that she might go off to Switzerland to meet Cal? Let alone get pregnant.

The party broke up half an hour later; all the way home, as the light on her bike picked out a small circle of pavement, and then the ruts in the lane, Joanna thought about babies. Rather than about sexy nightgowns.

She'd been a much-loved only child who'd longed for a sister or a brother, and who'd played, very traditionally, with dolls. She'd taken a baby-sitting course as soon as she was old enough, and in her late teens got summer jobs at play schools. She'd assumed that she and Gustave would start a baby once the honeymoon was over; and had battled with the bitterest of disappointments when he'd made it brutally clear he didn't want children.

He'd always begged the question before they were married, and in that tempest of longing and misplaced romanticism that had mesmerized her from the first moment she'd met him, she'd ignored this warning signal. After their marriage, Gustave had been unequivocal. *A couple of squalling brats? Not part of my life plan.* And then, as the months and years went by, she'd gradually become aware that she wasn't the only woman he was sleeping with. Tears, accusations, rage, none had had any effect. Or rather, they had had an effect: they'd driven her husband from her bed altogether.

She'd sometimes wondered if she'd outgrow this deep need to have a child. But she hadn't. If anything, as the years ticked by, the need grew stronger. She'd be twenty-nine her next birthday. Time was running out.

Joanna wasn't blind to reality. Having a baby wouldn't combine easily with writing; it would limit her options for part-time jobs and a social life. But none of this made any difference. She longed to be a mother, in a way that made nonsense of all her qualms.

The loss of the baby eight months ago had cut her to the quick. No matter that she hadn't loved the baby's father: her pregnancy had been the answer to a lifelong dream.

Tonight, hearing about Dianne's sister, she'd realized something else: that there were no guarantees. *Carpe diem,* Sally had said. Should she, Joanna, go to Switzerland, have an affair with Cal, and if she became pregnant, rejoice?

Could she do that?

Could she afford not to?

In the air-conditioned cool of Zurich's Kloten Airport, Cal was waiting at the arrivals gate. He was casually dressed in cotton trousers and an open-necked blue shirt. But he didn't feel casual. Anything but.

Joanna was due through the gate at any moment.

Would he ever forget that phone call, a few days ago, when she'd agreed to come to Switzerland? Even though she said she could only get away for four days because of her next group of students, the upsurge of pleasure he'd felt had been out of all proportion. But when he'd asked her why she'd changed her mind, she'd been downright evasive.

Well, he had four days to find out.

Was Plan D to seduce her?

Slow down, Cal. One thing at a time.

The first passengers trickled through. Over the babble of languages around him—Swiss-German, Italian, English, French—he swore he could hear the pounding of his own heart. Then he saw a tall, black-haired woman walk through the gate and hesitate for a moment, glancing around her as warily as a wild creature in an unfamiliar and threatening environment.

She was wearing raspberry-colored pants with a long, loose jacket over a purple camisole. Her hair was pulled back in a severe style that emphasized her stunning cheek-bones and slanted blue eyes; she looked both ravishing and remote. With a clenching of his nerves, Cal raised one hand in salute, easing his way through the crowd toward her.

She saw him immediately, and with none of her usual grace took a couple of steps toward him. Like Marie Antoinette on the way to the guillotine, Cal thought. "Joanna...lovely to see you," he said, contenting himself with kissing her on both cheeks, European-style. Her skin was cool; close up, her eyes were filled with primitive terror.

Terror? Did she regret her decision already?

"Jet-lagged?" he said lightly.

"Mmm...I didn't sleep well on the overnight flight to London. Then I had three hours in Heathrow, and now here I am. Not even sure what time of the day it is."

"We'll take it easy today, we don't have to get Lenny until tomorrow. Let's go find your bags."

He threaded her hand through his arm; her fingers were ice-cold. At the baggage carousel, Cal turned to face her. "Wishing you weren't here?" he asked, and watched her lashes flicker.

"I—"

"I'm very happy that you're here. You're on holiday, and all I want is for you to have a good time."

She made an indeterminate noise, staring absorbedly at his watch. "Is that Swiss?"

"Yeah." He tilted her chin with his fingers so she had to look at him. "Are you hungry?"

She swallowed, panic flaring in her irises. "I—plane food scarcely qualifies as food, does it?"

What the hell was going on? Apart from his hormones going on a rampage. That was a given. "I figured you might want to eat. So I made a reservation where we can sit outdoors and watch the world go by. Then we'll drive to my chalet near Appenzell and you can put your feet up and relax. The view's incredible and you won't have a thing in the world to do."

"Sounds great," she mumbled. "Oh look, there's my bag."

Cal picked it up, then guided her outdoors to the parking lot. He kept a sleek gray Jaguar for his use in Switzerland; as she settled herself on the leather seat, Joanna said, "You own this?"

"It's easier to keep a car here than rent one each time."

"I'll pay for lunch," she said edgily.

"You will not, and what's going on?"

"You paid my airfare, you don't have to pay for my meals, as well."

"You're here as my guest. And that's that."

Her lips were stubbornly set; he wanted to kiss them so

badly that he had to force himself to look away. Taking a couple of deep breaths, he set out to charm her, describing local landmarks as they drove into the city; earlier, Joanna had told him she'd never visited this part of the country. Flags snapped in the breeze. The River Limmat glittered under a cloudless sky, white swans drifting elegant and aloof on its polished surface. Rather like Joanna, thought Cal, and parked by the stone abutment. "We'll walk from here. Those spires are the cathedral, the Grossmünster, one of the best-known landmarks..." He kept talking, steering her toward Bahnhofstrasse, known as the most expensive street in Europe. He could sense her relaxing, her eyes wide as she took in the elegant stone facades of world-famous banks. Blue and white trams glided past stores offering designer jewelry, the latest in haute couture, leather handbags and handmade shoes. He said dryly, "You notice I'm not offering to buy you a present."

Her smile was almost natural. "Not even that taffeta gown with a waistline too small for Tinkerbell? I could wear it to weed the garden." Then she averted her eyes from an exquisite negligee displayed in solitary splendor behind plate glass, gazing instead at a trio of business-suited bankers. So was she as achingly aware of him as he of her? Cal wondered, and decided he wouldn't ask.

He'd like to buy her that negligee. Then he'd like to remove it from her body with leisurely sensuality...

He walked a little faster. Their table with its pristine linen cloth overlooked the river. Joanna watched the passersby with obvious fascination, tucking into a fondue made of three Swiss cheeses, accompanied by Kirsch. She followed this with a rich pastry drizzled with milk chocolate and filled with whipped cream. "Luscious," she said, licking her lips. "We'd better go for a brisk walk after this or I'll be asleep on my feet."

Obligingly he took her on a tour of the narrow streets of

Niederdorf, on the other side of the river, where she admired the medieval guild halls, the baroque Rathaus, and the galleries and boutiques of the Old Town; she bought chocolates for Sally and Dianne, carefully counting out her money. Under the shadow of the Fraumünster with its delicate spire, she gave a sigh of repletion. "I'm feeling better," she said. "But, you know, I'm really anxious to see the countryside, Cal."

"Then let's go," he said promptly, and again tucked her arm into his.

For a moment her fingers were rigid on his bare flesh. Then a flock of pure white gulls rose into the air from the river, and her eyes followed them, her fingers loosening. He had to make love to her while she was here, Cal thought, his mouth dry; but how could he, if she was this uptight?

Jasmine, Alesha and the rest had left him in no doubt that they were willing. Easy come and easy go, he thought grimly. Whereas Joanna knocked him off balance every time he looked at her and he had no idea in the world what she was thinking. Or feeling. Lenny, had she known about all this, would no doubt tell him it served him right.

Maybe Joanna was afraid to touch him. Afraid of the power of her own desire and where it might take her.

Maybe.

They drove east out of Zurich, Cal turning off as soon as possible onto lesser-traveled roads that wound through rolling green hills dotted with the sleek brown Simmental cows, brass bells jangling around their necks. Groves of dark evergreens climbed the slopes, amid whitewashed farmhouses and red-roofed barns. Cal talked on about the history of the area, and the prevalence of small family farms with their long-rooted traditions, finally stopping in exasperation to say, "I sound like a tour guide, for Pete's sake. Joanna, how *are* you?"

She sat up straight, giving him a wary glance. "Tired. Not quite here—jet travel's too fast, the rest of you has to catch up." She added less audibly, "Not at all sure I should be here."

"You're acting like I'm going to jump on you the minute we get to the chalet."

"Are you, Cal?"

"Dammit, no!" he exploded, and wondered who he was trying to convince, her or himself.

"Oh, look," she exclaimed as they turned a sharp corner, "mountains!"

A not very subtle change of subject from a woman entirely capable of subtlety. And he'd just publicly declared that he wasn't going to jump on her. So how was he going to seduce her if he couldn't even touch her? And what was wrong with him anyway? He was acting like a twelve-year-old instead of a grown man of thirty-six who knew the score. Or until today he would have thought he knew the score. "The highest one's called Säntis," he said, "we get a nice view of it from the balcony of my chalet."

Nice. A word he loathed.

Fifteen minutes later they drove through the little town of Appenzell, with its brightly painted, decorative houses, its window boxes crammed with geraniums, and its quaintly carved signs. A mile out of town, Cal took a driveway that wound up the hillside to a gabled wooden chalet. More window boxes, the blatting of the white goats that belonged to a villager, and a view that indeed he loved, for as always the mountains beckoned to him. "Well," he said tritely, "here we are."

The rest of the evening would long remain in his memory as one of the most excruciating in his life. He showed Joanna to the spacious guest room, the open window filled with the scent of roses that grew against the fence. He produced a credible meal of farmer's sausage and *rösti*, crusty potato cakes, along with a salad from his neighbor's garden. He talked. My God, how he talked. He even made her laugh once or twice. But by the end of the meal she was openly yawning. "Cal, I'm sorry. But I didn't sleep well last night, and I feel like I've been up forever."

"There's lots of hot water," he said, "feel free to have a shower. And get up whenever you feel like it in the morning." He leaned over and chastely kissed her on the cheek, keeping his arms at his sides with an effort that knotted his shoulders with tension. She stepped back faster than was necessary, smiled in his general direction and vanished down the hallway.

Seduction? That was the joke of the century. Plainly she was regretting her decision to come here; even more plainly, she was giving him the message that an affair was out of the question. So had he dreamed that kiss outside her cottage, the passionate generosity of her response, her shallow breathing and heated skin?

Whether he'd dreamed it or not, it was obviously a thing of the past. Not to be repeated. Joanna had come to Switzerland to admire the scenery, meet Lenny and take home some Swiss chocolate. Have a well-earned holiday, exactly what he'd promised her. And that, Cal Freeman, was that.

CHAPTER NINE

JOANNA woke at six-thirty in the morning, after a solid eight hours of sleep. She'd left the curtains open, and the pale pink light of dawn flooded the room. She got up and looked out. Wraiths of mist blanketed the valley; the early sun gilded the hills and the distant peak of Säntis. Somewhere close nearby a cow was chewing the cud, its bell a rhythmic accompaniment. The roses smelled delicious.

Without stopping to think, she pulled on some jeans and a sweatshirt, ran a brush through her hair and laced her sneakers. Then she crept down the hall and out the front door onto the veranda, where she filled her lungs with clean country air. Purposefully she set off down the driveway, goats scattering at her approach.

After her grand resolution to have an affair with Cal and start a baby, she'd spent the night alone in her double bed sleeping like a baby.

She wasn't even sure he wanted an affair. He'd acted more like her uncle, or a brother. Kissing her on the cheek, never once putting his arms around her, and talking nonstop. Speech could be a very neat ploy to keep someone at a distance and avoid all the essentials.

But then she hadn't been exactly honest when he'd asked her how she was. Asked with the kind of intensity that meant he'd really wanted an answer.

Tired, she'd said. Not really here. What she should have said was that her plan to get pregnant, which had seemed quite manageable in Sally's back garden with a bottle of wine on the table and Sally and Dianne encouraging her,

111

had revealed itself as utterly outrageous in the antiseptic cleanliness of the Kloten airport when face-to-face with the putative father.

She should never have come here. Just wait until she saw her two friends again. Friends, huh. Friends didn't talk you into nonsensical projects that you couldn't possibly carry out.

Cal didn't want her anymore. Had no plans to jump on her, to use his phrase. And wasn't that what really rankled? Although *hurt* would be a more accurate word for the way she felt.

She took a little path that meandered along the slope, yellow and white daisies nodding good morning to her. So was she going to spend this brief holiday bemoaning her undesirability? Or was she going to enjoy herself as much as she could?

The latter, Joanna thought valiantly, and concentrated on the stretch of her leg muscles and the pastoral beauty of her surroundings. An hour later, feeling wide awake and very hungry, she let herself in the front door as quietly as she'd exited. Cal must still be sleeping. She padded toward the bathroom in her socked feet, hoping she could find something for breakfast in the kitchen without having to open every cupboard.

The bathroom door swung open and Cal stepped out. With a tiny shriek of alarm, because she'd thought she was the only one up and about, Joanna walked right into him. Into his bare chest, into the towel swathed around his hips.

Into his waiting arms.

Heaven, she thought. Sheer heaven. And felt his arms tighten around her, fasten on her as if she were his heart's desire. He muttered her name, burying his face in her hair, raining kisses on her throat, pushing her shirt aside and tracing the line of her collarbone with his lips. Her whole body was engulfed in a wave of desire so primitive, so fierce, that she forgot everything but the delicious sensuality of Cal's mouth on her flesh.

She put her arms around his shoulders, caressing the tautly flowing muscles, the hardness of bone, the heat of his skin that smelled of pine-scented soap and of the man himself. As he pulled her roughly to his hips, she felt that other hardness with every nerve of her body. She wanted him. Here. Now. She wanted to know him in all the ways a woman can know a man, completely and without holding back anything of herself.

"Cal," she whispered, "oh, Cal, make love to me..."

He raised his head, his eyes boring into hers. "I want to. More than I can say...are you sure, Joanna?"

Her eyes shining, she said, "More sure than I've ever been of anything in my life."

He said roughly, "You're so honest. So generous."

"I thought last night you didn't want me anymore."

His laugh was wry. "I was thinking exactly the same about you."

"You *were?*"

"But I was wrong?"

That he should need reassurance moved her deeply. "We were both wrong," she said softly, and guided his hand to her breast. "Touch me, Cal..."

She hadn't bothered with a bra when she'd gone outside so early. She watched his face change as he traced the soft swell of her breast to its tip; then his mouth plummeted to hers as imperiously as an eagle falls from the sky.

She met him more than halfway, parting her lips to the demands of his tongue, making her own demands in a way new to her and utterly liberating.

Even now, before she'd made love with Cal, she somehow knew that he would welcome everything she was willing to give. So she opened to him, trusting him with both body and soul; as his hand roughly pushed aside her sweatshirt to smooth her bare skin, she said with only a touch of shyness, "This isn't fair."

He glanced at her, his smile weakening her knees. "What's not fair, darling Joanna?"

"You're only wearing a towel. But I've got clothes on. I happen to be a thoroughly modern woman who believes in equality."

"Plus the towel's slipping."

She looked down, blushed and said lamely, "So it is."

"In the interests of equality," he said, "I should take you to bed and remove every stitch you're wearing."

"Sounds like a plan," she said with a brilliant smile.

He swung her into his arms; as she linked her fingers around his nape, she said, "You have little black flecks in your eyes."

"I could drown in yours," Cal said. "Or clothe myself in your hair."

Shaken, she felt tears prick her lids. "That's a lovely thing to say."

He pushed at his bedroom door with his knee, kissing the sweep of her cheekbone. "I want you to know one thing—I'm not taking you to bed to have a casual affair. I don't know what you are to me—I'm being honest here—but there's something between us, I'd swear to it."

But Joanna didn't want talk. Especially talk about the future. She reached up, kissing him with lingering pleasure on the mouth, and saw the gray of his eyes darken to a storm of longing. Then he stooped, lowering her onto the crumpled sheets on his bed. "Last night I dreamed about you…and now you're here. In my bed."

"It's where I want to be," she whispered.

He dropped the towel to the floor. Fully naked, he leaned over, one hand on either side of her, and kissed her with passionate intensity. She pulled him down, exulting in his weight, his closeness, his very obvious hunger for her.

Their tongues danced, his tracing the soft curve of her lower lip, then plunging to taste all her sweetness. Her heart racing in her chest, she pressed the softness of her breasts against the hard wall of his chest.

He muttered, "You did say something about too many clothes, didn't you?"

She laughed, a carefree ripple of pure happiness. "What are you going to do about it?"

He raised himself on his palms. "Let me show you." Then, with barely restrained impatience, he tugged at the hem of her sweatshirt, raising it so the twin peaks of her breasts shone like ivory in the room's pale light. For a long moment he was silent. Then he said huskily, "I can't believe how exquisite you are. Tell me I'm not dreaming, Joanna."

"I'll show you," she said, and with a lithe twist of her body, sat up, pulling the shirt over her head.

Her hair, black as night, slid like water over her breasts, both hiding and revealing them. Cal took them in his hands, teasing the pink buds of her nipples, running his mouth over the firm rise of her flesh until she whimpered with mingled pleasure and need. Then he eased her back on the pillows, his fingers pulling down the zipper on her jeans and drawing them over her hips.

His eyes were fastened on her face. As he let his fingertips drift down her thighs, she gasped with delight, her hips arching upward. Lifting her in his hands, he stroked with lips and hands the arc of her rib cage, the curve of her waist and flare of her hips. Then he lowered his weight onto her, his chest hair abrading her breasts, his arousal heated and silky between her thighs.

He was ready for her. More than ready. What a fool she'd been to think he no longer wanted her, when every nuance of touch and impetus of desire now assured her of the contrary. As she moved her hips below him, aching to gather him in, words suddenly flashed across her mind. *I'm getting what I came here for: an affair with Cal. A possible pregnancy.*

The baby I've always wanted.

A baby had been the last thought in her mind the last few minutes. Briefly she turned her head away, closing her eyes, feeling as though someone had thrown ice-cold water in her face. As he'd carried her into his bedroom, Cal had been honest with her about his feelings. But she was about to deceive him. Use him for her own ends. Could she do that? Return truth with lies?

"Joanna, what's wrong? Did I hurt you?"

There was such concern in Cal's voice that of all Joanna's emotions, shame was uppermost. She couldn't do it. Much as she longed for a baby, she couldn't lie to Cal either in words or actions. He deserved better of her than that. She stammered, "I—I have something to tell you."

He reared up on his elbow, smoothing her hair from her face, tension tightening his jaw. "What is it, sweetheart?"

Sweetheart... She said rapidly, before she could lose her courage, "The reason I changed my mind about coming to Switzerland to see you—Cal, I'm so ashamed of myself."

"Tell me, Joanna."

She bit her lip. "Ever since I was a kid, I've wanted to be a mother. To have a child of my own. But Gustave didn't want children, although he didn't tell me that until after we were married. And on my next birthday I turn twenty-nine. So I decided I should come here and have an affair with you and perhaps I'd get pregnant—oh, God, it sounds so sordid, I'm sorry..."

His eyes narrowed. "What made you confess? Because I might as well tell you, birth control was the last thing on my mind."

"I couldn't use you like that," Joanna said in a low voice. "Or deceive you. It would be wrong."

He tilted her chin to the light, his gaze pinioning her to the bed. "So was all that an act?" he said harshly. "You were just pretending desire, so you could start a baby?"

"*No!*"

"Are you sure?"

"Cal, I swear to you I wanted you more than I ever wanted Gustave. I can't explain it, I don't understand it—but it's true. You think I'd have gone to bed with you otherwise?"

"I don't know...after all, what do I really know about you?"

The words poured out. "I've never gone to bed with anyone other than Gustave. I hated sex with him almost from the beginning, he was as selfish in bed as out. I couldn't have got this close to you without wanting you, of course I couldn't." She paused, frowning. "It would be like trying to write a book whose story I'd stolen from someone else, that didn't spring from my own imagination. Don't you see? Anyway," she added with a flare of spirit, "if I'd only cared about getting pregnant, all I had to do was keep my mouth shut."

He let out his breath in a small sigh. "I suppose so."

"I'm really sorry about all this," Joanna said painfully. "I'm going to get on the first plane out of here—I should never have come, I must have been out of my mind. And the last thing I should do is meet Lenny, that would be a disaster."

But Cal, she suddenly realized, wasn't listening; he had the air of a man who was thinking hard and fast. She sat up, grabbing for her shirt, wishing he'd pull the sheets over the sculpted lines of his torso with its pelt of dark hair and elegant curve of ribs. Confession or no, she still wanted him: her whole body was an ache of unfulfilled desire.

Not that she was going to tell him that. One confession before breakfast was more than enough.

He said in a peculiar voice, "You know, this could all work out for the best."

"I don't see how," she said. "I'm going home, Cal. Today."

"You could have a baby, Lenny could have a mother, and as for me—why, I could wake up every morning to find you in my bed."

A cold fist clamped around Joanna's heart. "What *are* you talking about?"

"Marriage," he said.

"Marriage?" she squawked.

"That's right. You and I. We'll get married. I'd be delighted to make a baby with you…and Lenny would love to have a brother or sister, she doesn't really like being an only child. I know she'll like you. She can come back to live in Vermont because you'll be living there, too, so that solves the problem of her homesickness. And you won't have to have part-time jobs because I'll pay off all your debts and support you—so you can write all the time. It works out perfectly, Joanna."

"But I don't want to get married!"

"Of course you do. You want a baby, don't you?"

"Haven't you heard of single mothers?"

"Not a good idea if there's a viable alternative," Cal said confidently. "Much better for the child to have two parents. That's one of the main reasons I've wanted to remarry, to give Lenny a stepmother."

A viable alternative. As if he were discussing the stock market, not the state of holy matrimony, thought Joanna in true fury. "You're not hearing me," she said crisply. "You might want to remarry. But I don't."

"I keep telling you I'm not Gustave!"

"Maybe not. Although how would I know until it's too late? I didn't find out what Gustave was like until after I was married to him."

"Then we'll live together for a while, if that'll make you feel better."

He had an answer for everything. Feeling beleaguered and horribly unhappy, Joanna hauled her sweatshirt over her head, saying in a muffled voice, "I'll probably never remarry. But I certainly won't marry another mountaineer. So that's that. Now let's phone the airline and have breakfast."

As she emerged from the folds of her shirt, she saw with another rush of fury that Cal was laughing at her. He said, "You look like a bantam rooster, all your feathers ruffled. Joanna, stop and think for a minute. All three of us—four, when our baby's born—can have what we want. It's so simple."

Our baby... Joanna smothered a pain so sharp that she almost cried out. She said in a hostile voice, "You know one thing that's wrong with this scenario? It's all about convenience. Nothing to do with feelings."

He rapped, "Don't tell me you didn't have any feelings when I was kissing you!"

"Love, Cal," she fumed, "I'm talking about love. You don't love me and I don't love you. So we can't possibly get married."

"You, I presume, were in love with Gustave when you married him...as I was in love with Suzanne. Gustave took you to the cleaner's, and Suzanne sure did the same to me. The kind of agreement we'd have would be much better than all this talk about love. Because that's all it is. Talk."

Joanna didn't have to be a mind reader to hear the pain underlying Cal's declaration. "How did Suzanne take you to the cleaner's?"

As he restlessly moved his shoulders, the muscles rippled across his chest. "She never grew up," he said. "She didn't want children, Lenny was a mistake. She just wanted me to climb mountains, play the stock market and leave her free to shop. Paris, London, New York, those were Suzanne's playgrounds, and in my heart I knew she wouldn't have been unhappy if I'd never come back from one of my expeditions. She'd have much preferred being a rich widow than a rich man's wife—all the fun and none of the responsibility.'' He added with a wry twist of his mouth, ''She also lied to me as often as she told the truth—one more reason I had trouble believing you back in January. I was like you, too young when I married to know the score.''

So Cal's marriage had been, in its way, as much of a wasteland as her own. ''I'm sorry,'' Joanna muttered inadequately.

''It's in the past. Over and done with.''

She wasn't so sure about that. ''Either way,'' she said carefully, ''I can't marry you. Not to have a baby, not for convenience, not for Lenny's sake. It wouldn't work, I know it wouldn't—I've had one bad marriage, I don't need another.''

''You're making a big mistake, you know that?''

''It's time you added the word *no* to your vocabulary!''

He grated, ''I've already told Lenny you'll be with me today, and you're not going to disappoint her. So you'll stay until Saturday as planned.''

Saturday was an aeon away, and how could she bear to be with Cal yet unable to make love with him? ''Tell her I had to fly home for an emergency,'' Joanna cried.

''I won't lie to my daughter for you or anyone else.''

She flushed. ''So I've got to act as though I'm delighted to be with you from now until Saturday? What's that if not a lie? She's smart, she'll know something's wrong.''

''The more I listen to you, the more I think you were acting your head off in bed. So to act delighted for a couple of days shouldn't be any problem.''

He couldn't have said anything more calculated to hurt.

"And a happy vacation to you, too," she retorted, swung her legs off the bed and got up. "I'm going to have a shower."

Cal, who had somehow maintained a formidable dignity while stark naked, made no move to stop her. Joanna stalked to the bathroom, locked the door and stared at herself in the mirror. So Cal thought she'd been faking desire: one lie on top of another. And once again, she'd been thwarted in her longing for a child.

She mustn't start to cry: because she might never stop. Joanna turned the water on cold and stepped in the shower. If she were writing this scene, there'd be a fadeout, and she'd find herself at the airport on Saturday without having to live through the intervening four days. She'd edit them out.

But unfortunately this was reality. She had to go out to the kitchen, eat breakfast with Cal and drive to Lenny's school.

How was she going to make small talk with Cal after her confession and his ridiculous proposal? And what if she really liked Lenny?

More to the point, Joanna thought, shivering as the cool water ran down her spine, how was she going to keep her hands off Cal?

Next time Dianne and Sally had an idea, she was going to run to her cottage, lock herself in and hide under the bed.

Bed...that word again.

A word she couldn't separate from another three-letter word. Cal.

CHAPTER TEN

SUNLIGHT filtering through handmade lace curtains, the scent of newly mown grass, the plaintive bleating of goats and the faraway clang of cow bells: the setting was idyllic, Cal thought, gazing out of the kitchen window at the blindingly white snow on the mountains. And he wished he were a thousand miles away.

With Joanna a thousand miles in the opposite direction.

Then the skin on the back of his neck prickled as he heard the pad of her approaching footsteps. He turned to face her. Her hair, whose midnight sheen had lain like silk over her naked breasts, was now held with a clasp on her nape; she was wearing a simple cap-sleeved dress the blue of the lobelias in his window boxes, sandals on her bare feet. Steeling himself, knowing it would be all too easy to refrain from admitting the truth, he rasped, "I shouldn't have said that about you acting in bed. I don't think you were."

Joanna stopped dead in her tracks. "You know what? You have a singular talent for taking me by surprise."

"Well, that's something," Cal said wryly.

"I was definitely not expecting you to apologize."

"I didn't apologize. I made a retraction."

"Oh, pardon me," she snorted.

He was starting to enjoy himself; especially when she added, "I certainly wasn't. Acting, I mean."

Her cheeks were fuchsia-pink. "You're sure not indifferent to me," he said slowly. "Guess I should be glad of that."

She was frowning at him. "I just figured something

out—I really hurt your feelings, didn't I? When I said I wouldn't marry you.''

Hurt, anger, frustration, desire: what hadn't he felt? ''I don't like rejection,'' Cal said. ''Who does?''

''You're not used to it,'' Joanna said shrewdly.

The words fell from his tongue without conscious volition. ''Suzanne never really liked sex. For her, it was part of the bargain—I got to have sex, she got to spend money.''

''So sex is a loaded issue for you, too. Truly I wasn't acting, Cal.''

''We'd better eat,'' he said brusquely. ''I don't want to be late for Lenny.''

She glanced at the table. Muesli, fresh strawberries and slices of cantaloupe, chocolate-coated croissants and a pot of delicious smelling coffee; she felt her throat tighten. In a rush she said, ''Gustave never once retracted anything he said, and he certainly never got breakfast for me—that was woman's work. And now I really will shut up.''

She plunked herself down at the table and reached for the pot of coffee at the same time as Cal. Briefly his hand overlaid hers; she stared with fascination at the tendons and white-scarred knuckles. He said in a strangled voice, ''You've got to stop doing that.''

''I took a cold shower—not that it did any good.''

''It'd take a couple of glaciers to cool me down.''

''Swimming in the Atlantic in January.''

''Scaling an Antarctic crevasse.''

She chuckled. ''I'm not *that* sexy. Pour the coffee...maybe caffeine will help.''

Since when had he laughed with a woman as much as with Joanna? And she was indeed that sexy. ''Did you know muesli was a Swiss invention?'' he said.

''I know it's very good for you, and if I eat a bowlful I can justify stuffing myself with croissants.''

He grinned. "A woman called Heidi makes them. Her husband yodels, just to complete the stereotype."

She helped herself to cereal and fruit, and for several minutes they chatted about the local economy. Then Joanna asked, taking a second croissant, "What have you told Lenny about me?"

"That you're the writer Ann Cartwright and the widow of a mountaineer. That's about it."

Lenny had been extremely curious about Joanna; but the more questions she'd asked, the more Cal had clammed up. He added, "Lenny writes poetry. I'm not sure which scares me more, poetry or puberty. Her real name's Ghislaine, by the way. But she started calling herself Lenny when she was three, and it stuck. Suzanne always called her Ghislaine, and made her wear frilly dresses...to this day, Lenny's something of a tomboy."

"I'm looking forward to meeting her," Joanna said. For wouldn't she learn more about Cal by seeing father and daughter together?

As though he'd read her mind, Cal said evenly, "I'm not retracting my proposal of marriage."

Her knife clattered on the plate. "Stop it, Cal."

"We get along well, we're attracted to each other and we could help each other out. Aren't those better reasons for marriage than undying love?"

The croissant suddenly tasted like paper. Joanna drained her coffee and stood up. "I'm going to clean my teeth. Then I'm ready to go."

"Think about it, Joanna. Think very hard."

"I bet sheer stubbornness got you to the top of all those mountains," she said nastily.

His jaw tightened. "I don't want us sniping at each other in front of Lenny."

"I'll be as sweet and gooey as a chocolate croissant."

"I mean it!"

"I promise that the—the impasse between you and me will not spoil your visit with your daughter."

"You're every bit as stubborn as I am."

"But not as arrogant."

"You're twice as sexy," he said, and watched unwilling amusement flicker across her features.

"I couldn't possibly be," she said, and fled the room.

They left ten minutes later, driving the short distance to St. Gallen through the lushly green countryside, then taking the narrow streets with care. The fifteenth-century houses, built to encircle the abbey, were lavishly decorated with gilt and brightly colored paint, full of Gothic charm. The abbey was famous for its sacred art and magnificently appointed library; the tolling of bells echoed among the rooftops. Lenny's school was just north of the town; a crowd of girls were gathered on the wide stone steps, and as Cal pulled up, one of them detached herself and came running down the steps toward them. Swiftly Cal got out of the car.

Lenny had a cap of gleaming brown hair, braces and Cal's gray eyes: that much Joanna saw before the girl flung herself into her father's arms. "Hi, Dad, great to see you, I'm so glad it's the last day of term and I can wear real clothes, not a uniform, and I've got a favor to ask you."

Cal swung his daughter into the air. "Great to see you, too. You're a half an inch taller than last time."

"For sure? I thought I was going to be short forever."

"Forever's a long time, Lenny," Cal said, and put her down on the ground again.

None of this was acting, either, thought Joanna; the affection between the two of them was very real. Her throat choked with emotion. Lucky Cal. If his marriage had been far from ideal, at least he had Lenny.

Then Cal said, "Joanna's in the car."

Hastily Lenny smoothed down her hair and tugged at her T-shirt. Oh, no, Joanna thought, she's nervous. Neophyte poet meets critically acclaimed author. She climbed out of the car and walked around to meet Lenny, her hand held out. "Hello, Lenny," she said with a warm smile, "I've heard so much about you. I'm delighted to meet you."

Lenny gulped. "Hello, Mrs. Strassen."

"Unless your father objects, I'd much prefer to be called Joanna."

"Fine with me," Cal said.

"Good," said Joanna. "You must be happy to be heading home, Lenny."

"I miss the farm, and my horse and the dogs and cats. And Dad, too, of course."

She, Joanna, by agreeing to marry Cal, could put an end to Lenny's homesickness. She said quickly, "You must tell me more about your horse...I used to have one when I was growing up."

"Horses were in your book."

"I have a feeling a lot of my childhood was in that book," Joanna said dryly. "A bit like undressing in public. Your father told me you write. If you like, we can talk about that, too."

"Oh, I'm not a real writer. Not like you."

"Everyone has to begin somewhere. And who says you're not a real writer?"

Lenny hesitated. "Me, I guess."

"Inner critics are the very worst kind."

Lenny was now gazing at Joanna with something like hero worship. Not quite sure how to deal with this, Joanna heard Cal ask, "What was the favor you wanted, Lenny?"

"My best friend Jan had to go home a week ago because she had the flu really badly. She's better now and wants me to go and stay overnight at her house before I go home. Her parents say it's okay. Can I, Dad?"

"Isn't that in Zermatt?"

"It's not that far."

"I'd have to see if we could get hotel rooms."

Joanna bit her lip, feeling suddenly frightened. If they went to Zermatt, it would mean another night in Cal's proximity, without the safety of Lenny's presence. Then Lenny said, "I bet you could—you've got all sorts of connections in Zermatt. There's a phone just inside the main door, Dad."

Cal's gaze met Joanna's and held it; she had no idea what he was thinking. He said abruptly, "That okay with you, Joanna?"

"Fine," she said brightly.

He took the steps two at a time. Lenny said, "Dad's kind of famous in Zermatt—he rescued four climbers who got in trouble on the north face of the Matterhorn when the weather changed. Dad went with the rescue helicopter and got them off the ledge, it was just about a blizzard. Dad hates to talk about stuff like that."

So Cal took risks. Big risks. No reason why that should upset her, all mountaineers took risks, it went with the territory. That he should be courageous in the service of others, Joanna chose to ignore. Discovering she didn't want to talk about Cal to Cal's daughter, Joanna said weakly, "I see," then changed the subject with a gaucheness rare to her. "What's your horse's name?"

Lenny chattered on for five minutes about all the animals on the farm; then Cal reappeared. "We're all set," he said, "let's get your luggage, Lenny."

The journey to Zermatt was so beautiful that Joanna ran out of superlatives. They drove due south at first, skirting the Austrian border and that of the little principality of Liechtenstein; then they turned west, following the Vorderrhein River past magnificent vistas of the Glarner Alps. They stopped for lunch by a tumbling mountain stream, its turquoise meltwater icy cold; a magpie scolded them from the spruce trees, the high peaks clothed in wisps of cloud. The Rhône valley led them further west until again they headed south along the Vispa. Dark chalets, houses as blindingly white as the snow on the mountains of Valais, the steep rocky gorge at Stalden; and then, finally, the short train trip to Zermatt.

"Jan'll meet us at that little café, Dad, on the main street," Lenny said as they disembarked. "We're early, though."

"We'll check in at the hotel first. Then we'll have time for a glass of wine at the café," Cal said. "Or else tea and pastries. Joanna has a sweet tooth too, Lenny."

Lenny had relaxed during the drive, Cal had noticed; and now was chatting to Joanna as if she'd known her for years. His intuition had told him that the two of them would like each other; he'd been right. Somehow he had to convince Joanna to marry him. Or at least live with him. She was a perfect choice from every angle that he could think of; he refused to believe that a few mountains and the ghost of her husband could get in the way. Or her insistence that the two of them should be madly in love with each other.

Love couldn't be trusted. They both knew that.

Once they'd checked in, they walked back to the café. Lenny and Joanna were ahead of him, Joanna's long, lightly tanned legs gleaming in the sunlight, her dress gently outlining the curves of hip and waist; her hair hung like a dark waterfall down her back. God, how he wanted her!

Tonight he'd be alone with her in the hotel. Was he going to move to Plan D? Do his level best to seduce her?

A horse-drawn carriage clopped past, and two of the ubiquitous electric taxis whizzed by. At the café, the roar of the river overlaid the guttural Swiss-German dialect; as they were led to their table, they could see the jagged tooth of the Matterhorn's summit rising from its wrap of cloud.

Then a man's voice called, "Cal, how are you? I didn't know you were in the area."

"Rudolf, good to see you—we just arrived," Cal said. "It's been a while…join us, why don't you?"

Rudolf, it transpired, was a member of the mountain rescue patrol; his eyes were very blue in his weatherbeaten face. "You must come and see our new helicopter, Cal," he enthused, "the very latest in technology. One of these days they won't even need pilots. Would the ladies excuse you for a short while?"

Lenny grinned, clearly entranced by Rudolf's courtly bow. As for Joanna, the less time she spent with Cal, the better. Being with him was like being presented with the biggest chocolate croissant in Switzerland and then being told you mustn't touch it. "Okay by me," she said.

"Sure," said Lenny. "Here's Jan's phone number, Dad. I'll be back at the hotel around nine tomorrow because the whole family has to go to Geneva in the morning."

"Have a good time," Cal said, kissing his daughter on the cheek. "Joanna, you'll be all right for a while?"

"I'll do some window-shopping," she said. "Why don't we meet at the hotel at seven?"

He leaned over and kissed her on the cheek, too. Subduing her shiver of response, she smiled at him sweetly. "Take your time, I'll enjoy being on my own."

His eyes narrowed. "I'll be back before seven."

As the two men threaded their way through the tables, Joanna noticed how women's eyes followed Cal's progress. And why not? He carried himself with an easy assumption of masculine power coupled with a kind of animal grace that was incredibly sexy. Why would she be the only one to notice him? He'd have no trouble finding a second wife and a mother for Lenny; the women would line up from here to the tip of the Matterhorn.

Joanna came back to earth with a bump as Cal's daughter said rather too casually, "Have you known Dad for long?"

"We met in January. But we've really seen very little of each other," Joanna said repressively.

"Oh." Lenny hesitated. "He never goes on holiday with anyone. Except me. So I kind of thought—"

"Lenny," Joanna said gently, "I think your father told you I'm a widow. My husband was also a mountaineer, he died on Annapurna last October. I don't really want to get involved with anyone right now."

Lenny's delicate features were screwed up in thought. "But maybe later?"

"I don't think so. You see, I found it very difficult being married to someone who was, in effect, married to the mountains. I was always afraid that he'd be killed...and then he was. So I'm not likely to choose another mountaineer for a husband—if that's what you're getting at." She smiled into Lenny's gray eyes. "Or maybe I'm jumping the gun. I just don't want you pinning your hopes on something that's not going to happen."

Lenny said naively, "I like you. Lots of adults say things like, *you wouldn't understand* or *you're much too young, dear.* You treat me like I'm grown up. Do you have any kids?"

Joanna fiddled with her cutlery. "No."

Lenny said with another of those outbursts of honesty, "I wish Dad would quit climbing. I get scared, too. Every time he goes. Although I've never told him because I don't want him to stop because of me. If you know what I mean."

"I know exactly what you mean."

Lenny frowned. "You know, it's funny but I don't remember my mother worrying much. She used to sing around the house when he was gone. And go out shopping lots. She was awfully pretty, not like me. She used to call me her little brown sparrow."

Joanna swallowed a rush of anger toward the unknown

Suzanne. She said calmly, "You'll be a Ghislaine before long, Lenny, you wait and see. Your eyes are beautifully shaped, and once your braces are gone and your face fills out a little, you'll be stunning."

"*Me?*"

"Yes, you."

"Wow." Lenny sat up a little taller. "But you're more beautiful than anyone I've ever seen...I'll never look like you."

"Nor should you—you'll look like yourself."

To Joanna's great relief, a tall red-haired girl suddenly hailed Lenny from the far side of the café. "Oh, there's Jan," Lenny said, and waved; Jan's parents were standing in the background. Lenny gave Joanna a blinding smile. "Thanks for telling me all that stuff. Maybe if we both work on Dad, he'll quit climbing." Then she grabbed her overnight bag and hurried to meet her friend.

Joanna watched them leave. So Lenny wanted Joanna as a stepmother; and hadn't wanted to hear how impossible that was. The trouble was, Joanna would love to be Lenny's stepmother; she'd warmed to Cal's daughter from the start.

One more reason she should never have come to Switzerland.

Joanna read for a while, drinking herbal tea and nibbling on yet more pastries. Time for a walk, or else she wouldn't fit into this dress anymore. Determined not to think about either Cal or Lenny, Joanna set off. The crowded main street fascinated her, with its classy boutiques where she did indeed just window-shop; she browsed happily in a bookstore for the better part of an hour, and avoided the shops carrying climbing equipment, although she couldn't as easily avoid all the climbers, some with harnesses and grappling hooks dangling from their waists. If it hadn't been for Gustave's climbing gear, she would never have met Cal...

She soon discovered the winding back lanes, where geraniums and fuchsias cascaded from the window boxes of the little chalets; after exploring there, she passed some more souvenir shops, wincing at the ubiquitous silhouette of the Matterhorn on everything from T-shirts to teapots; wandering further, she found herself at the gates of a cemetery.

A special cemetery, set apart for all those who had died on the mountain that dominated the skyline. Most of them men, many of them young.

As Gustave had been young. As Cal was young.

Cal. She gazed at the rough carving of a coil of rope on one of the headstones. What if something happened to Cal on his next expedition? What if he never came back?

How would she bear it?

She rested her fingers on the rough stone. She'd never see him again. Lenny would be left an orphan, and she, Joanna, would be—her thoughts slammed to a stop. Distraught? Bereft? Filled with a far deeper grief than the pain she'd felt for Gustave? Gustave had never honored the mountains with a matching honesty and integrity of his own. But Cal always would.

I'm not in love with Cal.

I can't afford to be in love with him.

I am in love with him.

CHAPTER ELEVEN

JOANNA stood very still, the headstone warming to her touch, her heart thumping as though she'd been running through the streets of Zermatt. Had she done what she'd sworn she'd never do, fallen in love again? With another mountain climber?

The thought of Cal being buried by an avalanche, lying broken-boned in a crevasse, or falling from a sheer rock face to his death: she knew too much about the very real dangers, and her imagination could supply the rest. Each of the infinite possibilities filled her with horror.

No, she thought frantically. Not Cal.

The stones, humped and weathered, wavered in her glance. The heat of the sun and the glancing shadows mocked her: for hadn't the cruelest of jokes been played on her? Once again she'd fallen in love with a mountaineer, a man in love with danger. But she could never tell him so, and she couldn't possibly live with him.

She had to get out of here. Her dark glasses hiding her eyes, Joanna stumbled out of the cemetery and back onto the street. She'd go to the hotel, where she could be alone. Out on the street like this, there were too many people and too much noise; and she herself was too far from home and all that was familiar and safe.

Blind to the allure of the boutiques, doing her best to avoid pedestrians, she took a wrong turn and found herself in the back streets again. Suppressing a whimper of pure distress, she stopped, trying to orient herself. The hotel should be to her right.

She hurried across the road, a couple of minutes later

seeing, far down the street, the elegant facade of their hotel. What she wanted to do more than anything was bury her face in her pillow and cry her eyes out. She couldn't do that: Cal was far too discerning. However, she could soak in a hot bath. Not exactly a cure for heartache. But it would have to do.

A woman pushing a baby carriage passed just in front of her, the baby peacefully sleeping, one little fist curled into its cheek. Like a knife to the heart, Joanna realized something else: that to bear Cal's child, loving him as she did, would make her the happiest woman on earth.

But she couldn't. Cal didn't love her, and he'd never agree to her raising his child on her own.

Tears filmed her vision. Frantic for privacy, Joanna lunged across the road toward the hotel, not even seeing the electric taxi racing up the hill. A horn assaulted her eardrums. Someone shouted a warning. She glanced sideways and made a leap for the sidewalk. But her toe caught on the curb. She tumbled forward, her knees and palms slamming onto the cool concrete. For an instant, she felt nothing. Then pain ripped along her nerves.

"Madame, permettez-moi…"

"Give the lady a hand up, now."

A small crowd had surrounded her. Italian and German added themselves to the chorus, and a man started lifting her to her feet. And then she heard the voice she least wanted to hear. *"Joanna*…what happened? Here, I'll look after her, thanks for your help."

Arms went around her, lifting her. Cal's arms. It was both agony and bliss to be held by him. The brass-ornamented doors swung open and closed behind her. An attendant offered more help in a tactful murmur, and then blessedly she was in the elevator, the doors smoothly shutting out the rest of the world. She faltered, "Let me down, it's nothing—"

"You've removed a fair bit of skin from one knee and I'm not putting you down until we get to our suite."

"I just want to be by myself," Joanna wailed, and to her horror started to sob as though her heart were broken. Cal tucked her head into his chest, marched down a paneled corridor and inserted a card into double doors that were painted with sprightly scenes of a medieval garden. Inside, he carried her straight to the bathroom, whose spotless mirrors presented Joanna with several reflections of a black-haired woman with bleeding knees in the arms of a tanned, broad-shouldered man. The woman was crying. Copiously.

Between sobs, she said fiercely, "Cal, go away!"

"No."

"I don't want you here."

"Too bad," he said, and lowered her into a gilt-edged chair covered with exquisitely embroidered tapestry. Then he reached up and pulled off her sunglasses. "What's the matter?" he said so gently that her eyes filled with tears again. "Don't cry, Joanna, I hate to see you cry."

"I feel so s-stupid, falling like that on the street."

"You don't know another soul here except me and Lenny, and we won't tell her a thing," he said comfortingly, meanwhile searching in his first-aid kit for disinfectant and filling the sink. "This probably reminds you of when you fell on the ice and lost the baby."

"Yes…yes, it does." Grateful for his understanding, she wrinkled her nose as he applied disinfectant; it stung enough to take her mind off everything else. She snuffled, "I won't be able to wear shorts for days."

"I'll order room service for dinner—a fall like that can leave you shaken up."

Cal was kneeling at her feet, smoothing on antibacterial cream, his lean fingers very gentle. His hair shone like polished leather under the lights; at the open neck of his shirt she could see the tangled pelt on his chest. She was stabbed by a desire so strong that she felt almost faint; of its own accord, her hand reached out and very lightly stroked his hair.

At that precise moment Cal looked up. She snatched her hand back. "I wasn't—"

He said hoarsely, "Joanna...sweetheart."

He lifted her to her feet, wrapped her in an embrace that felt like heaven on earth, and kissed her. Kissed her as he always kissed her, with passion and a desperate hunger that more than matched her own.

Afterward, she dimly remembered being carried into his bedroom with its huge bed and blue velvet drapes. She was never quite sure how they both got out of their clothes; but she did remember the heat of his naked skin on hers, his weight pressing her into the mattress. He muttered, "I'll be careful of your knees, my darling." And then neither of them said anything for quite a while.

Clinging to him as though she might fall were she to let go, Joanna ran her fingers the length of his spine, caressing his tautly muscled shoulders, kissing his mouth, his throat, his chest, and all the while achingly aware of his own explorations. Her breasts felt swollen, the nipples so sensitive that she cried out as he laved them with his tongue. Then he moved lower, parting her thighs, seeking out her other sensitivities. She was more than ready for him, engulfed in a storm of longing that would brook no delay. As a deep throbbing seized her, she felt him slide into her waiting warmth, filling her, so that her whole body was locked to his. Again she cried out his name.

His own throbbing leaped to meet hers, his face convulsing. But his eyes held hers, feeding on her release, allowing her to share his own so that she fell headlong into a pleasure that was overwhelmingly intense, an intimacy greater than she'd ever known. Nothing else in the world existed but Cal and herself, joined in the most primitive way possible.

Her heart was hammering in her ears: or was it Cal's heart? They were indistinguishable, she thought with sudden fierce possessiveness; and smiled at him with all her newly discovered love. "Oh, Cal," she said breathlessly, "I've never in my life been swept away like that."

"Nor I," he said huskily. "But it all happened too quickly, I shouldn't have been so—"

"I wasn't exactly telling you to slow down," she said. "No buts...it was perfect."

He gave her a lingering kiss. "How are your knees?"

Her laugh cascaded like sunlight on water. "Knees? What knees?"

But then, as though it were she who had fallen into a crevasse, she remembered her impetuous dash across the road, and her sudden fall. She sat bolt upright, her eyes wide with distress. "I know I'm the one who started this, you were so close and I wanted you so much—I just had to touch your hair, I couldn't stop myself. But I didn't plan it, truly I didn't."

Cal hesitated infinitesimally. "Plan it?"

"To get pregnant," she cried. "I'm not on the pill, and we didn't use any protection. But I swear it wasn't a setup."

"I didn't think you planned it," he said slowly, adding with the crooked smile she loved so much, "surely you've heard of spontaneous combustion?"

If anything, her distress deepened. She'd sworn to keep her distance from Cal and here she was naked in bed with him. That couldn't be called keeping her distance. And for all his endearments, she knew he didn't love her. He didn't believe in love. She pushed away from him, hauling the sheets up to cover her nudity. "We shouldn't have done this," she burst out.

"Joanna, we both wanted to. We're adults, neither of us involved with anyone else."

"Involved," she repeated bitterly. "What a cold-blooded word that is."

"Then if you prefer, we're neither of us in love with anyone else," he blazed. He reached for her, grasping her by the elbows and drawing her nearer to his body. "And now we're going to do it again. Taking our time."

To her utter consternation, desire spread a slow ache through her body. Already she wanted to make love with him again, she thought sickly, and struck him away. "You just don't get it, do you? I won't have an affair with you, Cal!"

"Then marry me."

The force of his will smote her like a blow. But that was all it was. Willpower. A rational list of all the reasons why she should marry him.

Nothing to do with love.

"I can't marry you. Or have an affair with you." Desperate to escape, she slid from the bed, grabbed her clothes, which were scattered all over the carpet, and clutched them to her chest. "There's nothing more to say, except I'm sorry we went to bed together, we shouldn't have…I'll see you in the morning."

With the speed and litheness of an athlete, Cal also stood up. He said with dangerous softness, "I won't force you, it's not my style. And I won't beg. Any more than I'll tell you I love you when the words are meaningless. But be very careful here, Joanna. You'd be a fool to deny what's between us."

"Sex. That's all it is."

"It's more than that, and you know it. It's some kind of elemental attraction that I've never felt before and that I don't understand—but I'm willing to go with it. All I'm asking is that you do the same."

"And what happens if I do?" she flashed. "Will you cancel your next expedition? Or will you head off to Annapurna leaving me home in dread of every phone call?"

"I don't take unnecessary risks on the mountains! I've turned back far more times than I've reached the summit—I'm not into the do-or-die stuff, believe me."

Which was, she realized, another source of his power: that he was confident enough of his masculinity to know when to turn back. "I won't do it to myself again," she said flatly. "For me to have an affair with you would be like heading for the summit in the worst blizzard of the century."

"For you to deny what's between us is to stay stuck at the base camp for the rest of your life."

"There's a difference between cowardice and learning from experience!"

"I said I wasn't going to beg, Joanna—and I'm not."

"I can't take this anymore," she said raggedly. "I'll meet you downstairs in the lobby at nine tomorrow morning."

Head held high, her clothes trailing on the floor in a loose bundle, she walked away from him; and with each step felt as though her heart were being torn in two.

She could have spent the night in his arms; he wanted her to, and didn't she crave to with every nerve in her body?

But at what cost?

Her bedroom adjoined the palatial living room; she opened the door and closed it behind her, the click of the latch as definitive as the final sentence of a book.

The End.

And what a horribly unhappy and ambivalent ending, she thought. But I can't edit it. It has to stay the way it is.

Sinking down on the bed, Joanna pressed her hands to

her face. Her skin smelled elusively of Cal. With a smothered cry of despair, she closed her eyes; never in her life had she felt so alone.

Cal woke in the middle of the night from a restless sleep punctuated with nightmares. The cry he'd heard—was that part of his dream or had it been real?

He lay still, eyes wide open, and heard it again. It was coming from Joanna's room, he realized, and surged to his feet. There couldn't be a break-in, the security in the hotel equaled that of the Zurich banks. But if someone was in her room, he'd flatten the bastard first and ask questions afterward.

He flung the door open and stood still, his eyes adjusting to the darkness. The room was empty but for Joanna; she was lying in a tangled heap of bedclothes and even as he watched, she gave another of those cries of utter desolation.

Pierced to the heart, he sat down on the bed and gathered her into his arms, cradling her head to his bare chest. Her nightgown, a concoction of silk and lace, was calculated to drive any man out of his mind. "Wake up, sweetheart," he urged, "you're having a bad dream."

Her eyes flew open, full of primitive terror. "Cal?" she whispered, pushing herself away from him. "*Cal?* But you're dead, I just identified the body…"

She thrust her fist into her mouth, biting hard on the knuckles. "It was in the morgue…they'd called me, Gustave had fallen from the Matterhorn. So I went there. But when they showed me the body, it wasn't Gustave. It was *you*…"

"I'm right here, Joanna," Cal said matter-of-factly. "I climbed the Matterhorn in my twenties and have no desire to climb it again. It was a dream, that's all. You're awake now and everything's okay."

"A dream," she repeated, as he reached over and smoothed her fingers flat.

"I was awake and I heard you cry out."

Her shoulders sagged. "What are we going to do, Cal? I can't be around you like this, it's too painful."

Suzanne had never showed him her pain; perhaps she'd never allowed herself to feel any. Even her final illness had been as swift and deadly as a heart attack, with no time for her to talk about her feelings. But Joanna was as open with her emotions as with her desire. Something tight-held shifted in Cal's chest; his one desire to comfort her, he said, "Just let me hold you for a while. Until you go back to sleep."

When he drew her toward him, she surrendered with a tiny sigh. The softness of her breasts heated his rib cage, her breathing teasing his shoulder with its elusive warmth. His reaction was entirely predictable, he thought ruefully. But he mustn't make love to her again. Because she was right: last time they'd used no protection.

If she got pregnant, surely she'd marry him.

He tried to banish these words. But they insisted on staying in the forefront of his mind. Were they true?

She'd said she'd raise a child on her own, as a single mother. But confronted with something other than theory— with a positive test result, with bodily symptoms and an actual delivery date—wouldn't Joanna think differently? Wouldn't she realize that an unborn child deserved two parents?

She placed a high premium on love. Just yesterday morning, in Appenzell, she'd said she didn't love him. Would that keep her from marrying him?

His thoughts were whirling in his head like a squirrel on a wheel. He tried to subdue his body's rampant response to her closeness, shifting a little so she wouldn't be aware of it. Then she looked up, her features a soft blur in the dim light. "You tear me apart, Cal...right now all I want is for you to make love to me. And yet we mustn't."

Only wanting to remove the strain in her voice, he kissed her awkwardly on the forehead. Then he started rubbing her shoulders, back and forth in a soothing rhythm. She cuddled into him with another of those small sighs, her hair lying like a length of dark silk over his forearm. Its scent reached his nostrils, mingling with the warm fragrance of her skin. Again he shifted a little. He'd pushed himself to his limits more than once in his life: but to hold Joanna in his arms and not make love to her was probably a greater challenge than any.

You can do it, he told himself. Sure you can.

Her hands, which had been cold when he'd first sat on the bed, had warmed now, curled into his chest like two small, trusting animals.

He couldn't abuse that trust. His shoulders tight with tension, his breathing shallow, Cal sat as still as he could. One leg was doubled under him, the cramping almost a relief because it took his mind off everything else. He dropped his cheek to the top of her head, letting his gaze roam around the room.

The red numbers on the digital clock by her bed changed with tantalizing slowness. Then, to his infinite relief, he realized Joanna had fallen back to sleep, her breathing subtly deeper and more relaxed.

He was safe. He'd wait a few more minutes, then he'd get out of here. With any luck she wouldn't even remember this in the morning. In fact, he hoped to heaven she wouldn't.

Making love with her earlier had blown his mind. Technique, timing, finesse, they'd all gone out the window, eclipsed by a raging hunger that—he now realized—had, deep down, frightened him. Because he'd been out of control.

Just as well Joanna had fallen asleep, he thought with a touch of grimness. These were deep waters that he'd do well to beware. Deeper than he'd expected. Far deeper; and more dangerous.

All he wanted was a good mother for Lenny, and a bedmate for himself. A companion. Certainly Joanna would never bore him; she was like the mountains in that respect.

What he didn't need was some kind of cataclysm in his life. Like falling in love. He'd done that once; and it hadn't worked. He wasn't about to do it again.

Besides, what was the point of falling in love with a woman who'd made it all too clear she didn't love him?

CHAPTER TWELVE

TEN minutes had passed since Joanna had fallen asleep. Moving very carefully, Cal pulled his thigh free, wincing as the circulation started up again. Then he eased her body down to the mattress. She murmured something in her sleep. Her hair slithered down his arm, running through his fingers and sliding onto the sheet. He'd like to see it in moonlight. He'd like it spread across his pillow every morning when he woke up.

With an exclamation of disgust, Cal straightened his other knee, the injured one that sometimes gave him trouble. As he rubbed it absently, Joanna twisted toward him, draping an arm over his other thigh; he was only wearing briefs. Her cleavage was a dark shadow; the swell of her hip made his fingertips itch to caress her. Then her eyes drifted open. He held himself like a statue, not even breathing.

"Cal?" she said softly, stroking his thigh with her hand, then resting her cheek against it. "To wake up and find you here...you feel so warm. So wonderfully familiar."

Go back to sleep, he thought, agonized. Because I can't take this anymore.

Then she pushed herself up on one elbow, smiling at him, her lips a soft, seductive curve, her eyes almost black. And Cal lost it. He plunged for her mouth. Taking her face between his palms, he kissed her as though there was no tomorrow. Only now.

Her response, fiery and overwhelmingly generous, inflamed every one of his senses. His control began to slide away from him, faster and faster. Slow down, he thought urgently. This time you can woo her, give her all the pleasure you're capable of.

Impregnate her?

He shoved that thought back where it belonged. This was about something else. Possession, certainly. Hunger, yes. But even more, it was about Joanna's needs. Wanting her happiness and fulfillment more than his own. Wanting to heal some of the wounds Gustave had dealt her.

With a feeling that he was scaling a peak he'd only dreamed of, and for which he might not be prepared, Cal gentled his kiss, wrapping her hair around his fingers. His tongue laved her lower lip. He drew her closer, the silk of her gown cool to the touch, her skin just as silky, infinitely desirable.

She felt fluid in his arms, pliant. Again forcing himself to move slowly, he pushed the straps of her gown from her shoulders, stroking the delicate bones, dropping his lips to trace their hollows and curves. Then he followed the sweet rise of her breast to its tip, her sharp indrawn breath all the encouragement he needed.

She found his own nipples, tangling her fingers in the rough hair on his chest. Suddenly impatient, she tugged at her gown, pulling it over her head and tossing it aside. Then she moved her hands lower down his body; with something of the same impatience, he rid himself of his briefs. She encircled him, his involuntary throb of response making her smile with a pride that touched him to the core. "Do that again," he whispered.

Then she lowered her head to take him in her mouth, her tongue circling where her fingers had been until he wondered if he could die from sheer pleasure. "You'd better stop," he gasped. "Besides, it's your turn, my darling."

He laid her back on the bed, her hair a black swirl, and rested his weight on her, kissing her lips, the long tendons of her throat, the swollen peaks of her breasts. Drinking in her beauty, from the taut belly to the nest of dark hair at the juncture of her thighs, he covered her with his kisses, setting his seal upon her, the seal of possession. She writhed beneath him, her hips lifting to take him in, her breath coming in short gasps as he played with the soft petals of wet, warm flesh where she was most sensitive to his touch.

But Cal was in no hurry. He rolled over, carrying her with him, her body boneless in his hands. Then he lifted her to straddle him, taking care not to jar her sore knee. As he slid into her, her face changed. She said urgently, "Now, Cal, now…"

He thrust upward, clasping her around the waist, the firm rise of her breasts as erotic as the host of other sensations that claimed him in all their inexorability. But even then he was stroking her between the thighs with all the skill at his command, watching the tension gather in her face. Her head bowed, she gasped his name, then cried out in a passion of release.

Only then did Cal allow himself his own release, an abyss of mingled pain and pleasure that carried him deeper and further than he'd ever been before. Distantly he was aware of her heels gripping his thighs, her hands smoothing the tangle of hair on his chest. And realized he'd been saying her name over and over again, wanting time to stop with Joanna and him as one.

With exquisite grace, she lowered herself to lie across his chest; and in another of those pangs of tenderness, Cal felt the racing of her heart against his breastbone. He wrapped his arms around her. "Darling Joanna…"

She made a tiny sound of pure contentment. "I know you're not supposed to make comparisons," she murmured drowsily, "it's not good etiquette. But you took such care of me—that's never happened to me before."

Gustave, in other words, had looked after himself rather

than his wife. In bed as well as out. Cal said, "Suzanne never liked sex. Too messy, too real, too—naked, I suppose."

"Were you faithful to her, Cal?"

"Yeah…part of the deal."

She raised her head. "So you liked what we did?"

There was a touch of uncertainty in her voice. "Liked it?" he repeated. "Oh, yes, I liked it. The earth moved, isn't that the current cliché? Well, let's say the Matterhorn moved."

"Just the Matterhorn? Not the entire Alps?"

He wanted to say, *Next time we'll go for the Alps.* But something stopped him. "How about the Himalayas?" he offered, and heard her chuckle sleepily. Again she rested her cheek on his chest, closing her eyes with a sigh of repletion. Cal lay very still. Within moments she was asleep again, the fingers of her left hand curved to his ribs, of her right curling around his shoulder.

This was what he wanted. Joanna in his bed. Making love with her, sleeping with her, waking in the morning to find her in his embrace.

He was happy, Cal thought incredulously. Filled with happiness, pure and simple. Light-headed with happiness. Wasn't that partly why he climbed, in search of a joy he'd never found in the arms of a woman?

Until Joanna.

What if she were pregnant? What then?

Joanna woke gradually, to a delicious lassitude and the heat of a man's thigh lying against her own. An arm lay heavily across her hip. In a flash it all came back to her: the tumultuous love-making in Cal's bedroom, her flight to her own room, the nightmarish images of a dead climber who was the man she loved…and then that other, dreamlike lovemaking, slow and infinitely erotic.

Only a few hours ago, she'd sworn she wouldn't have an affair with Cal. And now she'd woken in his arms.

He was a wonderful lover, passionate and attentive, totally focused. She'd never felt such a pitch of arousal, or such incredible fulfillment.

And now it was over. Lenny would be back this morning, and two days from now she herself would get on a plane to fly to London. How long before she'd wonder if she really had dreamed this night in Cal's arms?

Her lashes flickered. Again they'd used no protection. And it was—she'd known this before she left home—the most fertile part of her cycle.

Perhaps she was pregnant.

The mere possibility filled Joanna with a tumult of emotions, so that she could scarcely breathe. Hope like sunshine after a storm, joy like an opening rose; and the utter despair, the blighted rose, of knowing that the father of her child would never fall in love with her. Wouldn't allow himself to.

Valiantly she pushed all the emotions down. She couldn't afford them. Not now. Not when she had to spend the day with Cal and Lenny. Besides, it was very unlikely that she was pregnant. Raising herself cautiously, she peered at the digital clock beside the bed.

Eight forty-five. She blinked, wondering if she were dreaming again. But even as she watched, the last number changed. Eight forty-six.

Lenny was due back at the hotel at nine. With a yelp of alarm, Joanna scrambled out of bed. Cal turned over in his sleep, reaching for her. Then his eyes opened, and he stretched luxuriously. "Joanna?" he mumbled. "Come back to bed."

"It's quarter to nine! Lenny'll be here any minute."

He reared up on his elbow, raking his hair back. "Are you kidding? I never sleep past seven."

"You just did. I'm going to have a shower."

She ran for her bathroom and locked the door. After the quickest shower on record, she hurried back into the bedroom, which was mercifully empty, and dressed in her tunic top over a camisole, along with loose trousers that hid her scraped knees. Her hair she gathered in a knot on the back of her head; huge purple and pink earrings would, she hoped, distract from the faint blue shadows under her eyes.

Not once did she look at the bed.

Her sandals were in the living room. She pulled them on and slapped on some makeup to the sound of Cal's razor. "I'll meet you in the dining room," she called, and ran for the elevator.

So when Lenny appeared in the archway of the elegant dining room, with its splendid view of the hooked Matterhorn, Joanna was peacefully reading a book. As Lenny sat down across from her, Joanna said smoothly, "Your father should be down any minute. Did you have a good time with Jan and her family?"

Then, with a lurch of her heart, she saw Cal come through the archway and stride toward their table. Formidable, she thought. That was the word that most truly applied to him. And braced herself to act like a platonic friend and not the woman who'd spent a night of passion in his arms.

He hugged his daughter, smiled at Joanna as impersonally as if she were indeed nothing but a friend, and said cheerfully, "I'm starving. Have you eaten, Lenny?"

And somehow that set the pattern for the next three days. It would have been very difficult for Joanna to have staved off advances from Cal; it was totally disconcerting to have him act as though she scarcely existed. Nevertheless, she stayed close to Lenny, who, not very subtly, kept trying to leave the two adults alone. Cal smiled a lot, with the air of a man having a pleasant holiday with his much-loved daughter and a female acquaintance who just happened to have joined them.

They hiked around the Saas villages, discovering a path set with fifteen white chapels, sighting the glacier and the peak of the Dom; every mountain seemed a cruel reminder to Joanna of what she couldn't have. They stayed in a delightful chalet that night. The next morning, they drove to Montreux, eating lunch on the shore of Lake Geneva, the patio of the restaurant surrounded by rose-pink camellias and the rustle of palm trees. Lenny, who had been exposed to Byron in her English class, wanted to see the Château de Chillon; after a short boat trip, Joanna saw the towers and high windows of the castle, where a sixteenth-century prior had been chained for six years in an underground dungeon. Lenny had a ghoulish wish to see the dungeon; Joanna stayed behind in the Great Hall with its magnificent frescoes.

She had no desire to see a dungeon. For wasn't she a prisoner? she thought painfully. A prisoner of her past. And surely Cal was the same. Long ago, he'd fallen in love with a woman who, by all accounts, had both used and disdained him. So he'd lost faith that real love could exist between a man and a woman.

Tomorrow couldn't come soon enough.

Cal drove fast all the way to Bern, where they stayed in a charming centuries-old hotel. As soon as they'd eaten a late dinner, Joanna gave an exaggerated yawn. "I'm off to bed," she said with a smile that felt as though it was stretching every muscle in her face. "See you both in the morning."

She ran upstairs, bolted herself into her room, and fell into bed. All she had to do was keep Cal at bay for one more day. Then she'd be safe.

Not that she'd had to keep him at bay: he'd made no attempt to be alone with her. Was he biding his time? Was he so scrupulous a father he wouldn't allow even the slightest hint to his daughter that he could be involved with Joanna? Or had he—since she'd surrendered so ardently to him—lost interest in her? Perhaps she was like the Matterhorn, she thought with a nasty jolt: once climbed, he'd lost interest in it.

She slept fitfully, went for an early and solitary walk in the lanes of the old city, where the ubiquitous clock faces did little to comfort her, and was back for breakfast before Lenny was up. Cal was sitting alone in the dining room. Steeling herself, she went to join him.

He looked at her unsmilingly. "Lenny'll be here any minute," he said in a clipped voice. "I've purposely kept my distance the last few days, Joanna. It seemed the best way to handle the situation with Lenny around—we sure as hell couldn't sleep together. But once you've finished with your next group of students, I want you to visit us in Vermont. You can get a feel for the place...see us on our home turf."

"Do you love me, Cal?" she said deliberately.

His jaw hardened. "I told you how I feel about love. It doesn't last."

"Then the answer's no—I won't come to Vermont."

"Do you love me?"

She should have seen that coming. She said, choosing her words, "I, too, have learned that falling in love doesn't guarantee happiness. We're both prisoners. Just like that man Bonivard in his underground dungeon."

"What if you're pregnant?"

"I doubt that I am."

"Answer the question, Joanna."

"I'll manage."

Sheer fury darkened his eyes. "You'll manage," he repeated in a savage whisper. "This isn't just your child we're talking about—it's mine, too."

"Perhaps you should have thought of that before you made love to me."

"You said it wasn't a setup!"

"It wasn't. You were there, you know what happened."

He grasped her wrist with punishing strength. "If you're pregnant, you must let me know."

"You're hurting," she seethed. "Let go!"

With insulting speed he let her hand drop back on the cloth. "You'll let me know, Joanna."

"All right," she snapped, "I will."

He leaned back in his chair. "Smile," he said mockingly, "Lenny's coming."

"It's a wonder to me no one's ever pushed you off a mountain face."

"I'll have to make sure I never take you climbing," he said with a lazy grin that she itched to remove from his face. "Hello, hon," he added, "how did you sleep?"

Lenny smiled at Joanna. "Dad took me for an ice cream after dinner, down by the river. We saw all these incredible clocks with bears on them, you should have come, Joanna."

Joanna produced some kind of reply, and buried her face in the menu. Only seven more hours, she thought. Then she'd be winging west to London, where she'd make her connection for the transatlantic flight. Back home.

Those seven hours, which began in Bern and ended in Zurich, were never very clear in Joanna's mind. They drove through the Jura, with its ripening vineyards, sloping farms and sleekly handsome horses. Lunch, a meal for which Joanna had no appetite, was in Solothurn near the cathedral. Her nerves were tightening to an unbearable pitch; just to glance at Cal filled her with an agony of regret. Yet she was sure she was doing the right thing: a clean break now was better than prolonging a relationship that was doomed to be one-sided.

They skirted Zurich, driving straight to the airport. Once Joanna had checked in, Lenny said overly brightly, "Goodbye, Joanna…please come for a visit."

Joanna kissed the girl on the cheek. "It was lovely to meet you, Lenny," she said evasively. "Good luck with your writing."

But Lenny could be as persistent as her father. "Be sure and give Dad your address. Then I can send you some of my poems, that'd be okay, wouldn't it?"

"Yes," Joanna said weakly, "that would be fine."

"I'm going to get a magazine, Dad, I'll be over at that kiosk."

So what Joanna had hoped wouldn't happen had happened: she was alone with Cal. She said rapidly, "My box number is 183, in Harcourt."

"And I already have your phone number." He rested his hands on her shoulders; to her overwrought imagination, they felt heavy as boulders. "Marry me, Joanna."

As she flinched, shaking her head, he added with ruthless certitude, "I'm not going to go away."

"You've got to."

"I'll call in a month or so to find out if you're pregnant. Lenny really likes you, you know that."

She said in a low voice, gazing at the buttons on his shirt, "I beg you not to use Lenny as a weapon…if you have any feelings toward me at all, just let me go."

"Oh, I have feelings toward you."

He didn't look remotely loving, she thought with an inward shiver. He looked more like he hated her. "I have to go through security," she said jaggedly, "I want to pick up a couple of bottles of Swiss wine in the duty-free."

He glanced over his shoulder; Lenny was absorbed in reading a magazine, her back to them. Taking Joanna in his arms, Cal lowered his head and kissed her with a powerful mix of fury, possessiveness and passion.

For a moment Joanna was petrified. Then her fighting spirit rose to the surface. She could go out with a bang or a whimper, she thought, and kissed him back with all her pent-up frustration and unhappiness. But all too quickly those emotions turned to desire, a desire she was helpless to resist. Melting into his arms, she laced her hands around his neck and surrendered herself to a tide of sensation.

Abruptly Cal pushed her away. His eyes like stones, he rasped, "You have feelings for me and don't bother denying it. I'll be in touch." Then he strode across the terminal toward the kiosk.

Joanna took her boarding pass and passport out of her bag with fingers that were shaking like poplar leaves, and followed the signs to security.

Security. What a laugh.

But at least she was going home. Home where she belonged.

CHAPTER THIRTEEN

EARLY August, and one of those days that proved summer a misnomer. Joanna came out of the doctor's office and started walking along Harcourt's main street, her head bent against the wind and rain. She'd planned the appointment so that no matter what she found out, she wouldn't have to go back to the campus and face any of her students or co-workers. So now all she had to do was get her bicycle from the car park where she'd locked it to the bike rack, and cycle home.

The weather perfectly suited her mood. The last few weeks had been the worst in her life: worse than last October when she'd miscarried; worse even than that long-ago summer when she'd finally realized that Gustave had no intention either of being faithful to her or of giving her a baby.

She missed Cal unrelentingly, his absence like a gaping wound in every moment of every day. Not that she was allowing her misery to show. Rather, she was carrying on with her classes, seeing Sally and Dianne, shopping, going to the occasional movie, working in her garden. Just like normal.

Except that nothing about her days—or nights—felt normal. Not even now, when Cal had at last stopped phoning her. Three times in the first week after she'd returned from Switzerland it had been his voice on the end of the line when she'd picked up the phone. So she'd threatened to change to an unlisted number, and the phone calls had stopped.

But now she had to phone him.

155

Raindrops were clinging to the handlebars of her bike. She undid the padlock, got on the bike and turned onto the street. The swish of the tires on the road was oddly comforting; she had to pay attention to the puddles and the oncoming traffic, and that, too, was a good thing. Then on the lane it was a question of avoiding the worst of the mud.

It had been raining the day Cal had come to Harcourt, and followed her down the lane; the day he'd kissed her by the apple tree in front of all her students.

Cal. Father of her child.

For, of course, she was pregnant. She'd been almost certain she was for the last three weeks, and today's visit with her doctor had confirmed it. At long last she was to realize her desire to become a mother.

So why wasn't she delirious with joy? Hadn't she gotten exactly what she'd wanted when she'd gone to Switzerland to be with Cal?

She wobbled down the rutted lane, the leaves on the hedges flailed by the wind, clouds skudding across the sky. When she'd set off for Switzerland, she'd only planned on getting pregnant; not on falling in love with Cal. Or had she already fallen in love with him and simply not realized it, blind to all the signs? Either way, it made no difference. He had feelings for her. So he said.

Sexual feelings, she thought. The possessiveness of a powerful male. But not love.

She couldn't marry him. And that was the stance she had to stick to when she phoned him this evening.

Her little cottage was dank and chilly. She flipped on the electric heat, made herself some supper, and did her best to ignore the pile of papers on one side of her desk: poems that Lenny had sent her. Astonishingly good poems, given Lenny's age and lack of experience. Lenny had ended her last letter to Joanna by saying that her father was stomping around the house like a bear with a head cold and she hoped

Joanna would come for a visit soon: a naive comment that had caused Joanna to wish Lenny would stick to writing poems, rather than letters.

Cal hadn't written to her. But then, why would he?

The clock crept toward six, when the phone rates went down. At two minutes past six, Joanna picked up the receiver and dialed Cal's number, praying that he'd answer rather than Lenny, simultaneously praying that he was in Kathmandu.

"Cal Freeman," he said, sounding very business-like.

She took a deep breath, realizing in a panic that she should have rehearsed what she was going to say. "Hello?" Cal repeated sharply.

"Cal, it's Joanna."

There was a noticeable pause. Then he said in a voice like surgical steel, "Are you pregnant?"

How typical of the man that he go straight to the essentials, she thought in a spurt of rage. "Yes."

Another pause, so long that she couldn't bear the silence. "I just found out today," she added.

"I'm coming up to see you."

"No! No, you mustn't."

"Joanna, I'm the father of your child. We have to talk about the future. When we'll get married."

Her palm wet on the receiver, she said, "We're not getting married."

"I'm not having a child of mine brought up in penury."

She played her trump card. "My second novel was accepted last week by a major publishing house in New York. I'm getting a six-figure advance. So I don't need your money."

"I guess I should be congratulating you on two fronts," he grated. "You achieved your aim in coming to Switzerland and you're obviously launched on a very successful career. But you'll forgive me, I'm sure, if I say I don't feel congratulatory.'' His breathing harsh, he went on, ''Okay, we'll skip the money angle. You think I'm going to put up with my son or daughter being brought up illegitimate? Do you know how cruel kids can be in the schoolyard—is that what you want?''

''Of course not.'' Her brain seemed to be on hold; she faltered. ''You knew I wanted to get pregnant. You shouldn't have made love with me.''

''You think I had a choice?''

She knew exactly what he meant. ''Even the second time, we didn't use protection.''

''Did it ever occur to you that I thought about that at the time, and was stupid enough to believe you'd marry me if you got pregnant?''

It hadn't occurred to her. ''That *was* stupid of you.''

''I'll book a flight as soon as I get off the phone. I can be there tomorrow.''

''Cal, you're not invited! I don't want to see you. Tomorrow or next week or next year. I'm on my own with this baby and that's the way I want it to be.''

''But it's not the way I want it to be.''

''If you come up here harassing me, I'll move in with my friends. Or I'll report you to the police.''

''You hate me, don't you?'' Cal said in a voice empty of emotion. ''You're right, I am stupid—it took me this long to see it.''

''Of course I don't.''

''So what is this, some kind of posthumous revenge on Gustave?''

Worse and worse. ''I don't play games like that.''

''Then what kind of game are you playing?''

''It's your old problem, Cal—you don't want to hear the word *no*. No, I don't want to see you. No, I don't want your money. No, I don't want to marry you.''

''Yet you want my child.''

"I've wanted a child for as long as I can remember."

"A child. Any child will do. Thanks a lot, that really makes my day."

"Oh, stop!" she cried. "You're poisoning everything. I won't marry you—I won't!"

An inimical silence echoed down the line. "And that's your final word?"

"Yes," she said; and wondered how one small word could make her feel so horribly unhappy.

"In that case, I'll speak to Lenny this evening," Cal snarled, "and tell her I don't want her communicating with you anymore. And you won't get in touch with her, do you hear me?"

What had she expected, that she'd be able to cut her ties with Cal and keep them with Lenny? Have her cake and eat it, too? "Very well," she said tightly.

"Goodbye, Joanna."

The connection was cut with a decisive click. Joanna dropped the receiver as if it were red-hot, sank into the nearest chair and gazed unseeingly at the wall.

An hour after Cal finished talking to Joanna, the phone rang again. He snatched it up, convinced she'd changed her mind, his heart racing as if he were twenty-thousand feet up a mountainside. "Joanna?"

"Cal? This is your old friend Ludo Galliker. I am calling you from Grindelwald."

Not Joanna. Well, of course not. She wasn't the type of woman to say she never wanted to hear from him again and then pick up the telephone half an hour later. "Ludo," Cal said, trying to pull himself together. "How are you?"

Really original, Cal. Brilliant.

"I am well, thank you," Ludo said with the formality that he favored when on the phone. "I thought I should get in touch with you…in case you hadn't heard about Tony Mason.''

Tony had been on the Everest and Kongur expeditions with Cal: an experienced and canny climber, whose store of off-color stories had often entertained them in their tents high on the ridges. "What's wrong?" Cal asked, apprehension stretching nerves already pulled taut.

"An icefall on Brammah. I only heard because my nephew was on the same expedition. It happened two days ago." He went on to give a few technicalities about location.

"I'm so sorry," Cal said. "He was a great guy—and such a good climber."

"Good climbers die, bad climbers survive, sometimes it's just a matter of luck…you are in the wrong place at the wrong time and no skill in the world can save you," Ludo said. "That's one reason I do very little climbing now. Lady Luck—isn't that what you Americans call her?—she doesn't like to be pushed too far."

Cal knew there was more than an element of truth in this. On several of the expeditions he'd been on, luck had run out for one or more of the climbers, men whose judgment and skill he had deeply respected. He said heavily, "I'm glad you let me know."

There was a brief pause. "If you don't mind me asking," Ludo said, "did Joanna Strassen forgive you?"

"I asked her to marry me. She won't."

"Ah…so the wounds went deep from Gustave—I'm not surprised," Ludo said, adding dismissively, "Well, it was worth a try. And it's not the end of the world, there are lots of other women."

Cal didn't want any other women. "Yeah," he said, "of course there are. How's the arthritis?"

They talked a few more minutes, then Cal hung up. His own luck had run out today, he thought. He'd been so sure

Joanna would marry him if she were pregnant. But he'd been wrong.

Maybe he'd been wrong about her all along. Maybe she'd simply used him for her own ends, and now that she'd gotten what she wanted, he was of no further good to her. Useless as a frayed harness.

He sure hadn't realized what Suzanne was like when he'd first met her; he'd been blind as the proverbial bat.

But he'd been in love with Suzanne. He wasn't in love with Joanna.

Distantly he heard the sound of a vehicle on the gravel driveway: Lenny, back from practising for the local horse show next week. He'd better start acting like a human being.

"Dad?" she called. "Hey, guess what, Dad?"

Lenny would soon have a half sister or brother, he thought. But he couldn't tell her that. Now or ever. He called back, "I'm in my study."

She burst in the door, her cheeks pink with excitement. "I jumped Lara twice over the water hazard, and she did just fine. Then we topped four feet six on the bars."

"That's great," Cal said.

"And I had a letter from Joanna today, critiquing my poems, she thinks some of them are good." Lenny gave a sigh of pure bliss. "What a fab day."

He'd better tell her now. What was the point of delaying it? He said, "Lenny, there's something I have to tell you."

Lenny's smile died. She said slowly, "You don't look so hot. What's up?"

"I'd rather you didn't get in touch with Joanna again. And I've told her the same."

"Why not?" Lenny asked blankly.

"I'd hoped she might marry me, but she won't," Cal said, trying to erase any trace of feeling from his words. "So I think it's better we cut the connection completely."

"It's because you're a mountaineer—that's why she won't marry you."

"She doesn't love me," Cal heard himself say, and instantly wished it unsaid. Love. He didn't believe in it. Except for his love for Lenny, of course.

"She's scared to. Her husband was a mountaineer, she told me about him, he was killed on Annapurna...if you quit climbing, I bet she'd reconsider. She liked you, I could tell."

"I don't think it's that simple."

"Why don't you stop climbing?" Lenny blurted. "You've done all the big ones."

Cal said reluctantly, "I just had a call from Ludo that one of my climbing buddies was killed in an icefall on Brammah a couple of days ago."

"Oh." His daughter's face was suddenly pinched. "So when are you going again, Dad?"

Soon. The sooner the better. "I don't know, I haven't—"

"I wish you'd quit, too," Lenny said almost inaudibly.

"Lenny—did you say what I thought you said?"

"I've wanted you to quit for ages!"

"You do? You've never said so before."

"It's like Joanna said," Lenny went on in a strained voice. "Always waiting for a phone call, afraid to pick it up, knowing people die just because they're on the mountain. Is that what happened to your friend?"

"Yeah...but Lenny—"

Lenny's jaw set mulishly. "Anyway, I don't want to stop writing to Joanna! I really like her, and I'm sure she likes you. If only you'd give up climbing, I bet she would marry you."

"Lenny, I don't often lay down the law. But this is one case where I'm going to. I don't want you to keep in touch with Joanna."

Tears filmed Lenny's gray eyes, that were so like his own. "So climb your stupid mountains, see if I care!" After this unusually childish outburst, she ran from the room. A couple of moments later Cal heard her bedroom door slam.

How could he quit climbing? And what if Lenny disobeyed him and somehow found out about Joanna's pregnancy? For which he was at least half responsible.

What would he do then?

He rued the day he'd driven along a prairie road in a blizzard and stopped to rescue a stranger. A woman who'd turned his life upside down. A woman who didn't want to be with him, even though he was the father of her child. Was he going to spend the rest of his life hankering after a black-haired beauty who had all kinds of hang-ups about love and children and mountains?

It's not the end of the world, there are lots of other women... Was Ludo right?

CHAPTER FOURTEEN

AUGUST was passing, progressively more hot and humid. Physically Joanna was feeling very well; emotionally she was a basketcase. The latter she kept to herself as best she could. Last night over chips and salsa she'd told Sally and Dianne about her pregnancy, certain that they'd support her in her wish to be a single mother. But neither of them had. Worse, they'd argued with her vociferously. So she'd had a rotten night's sleep, and woken from a dream in which Cal's arms were wrapped around her.

Her bed had been empty, her heart one big ache.

Five in the afternoon. Yesterday her classes had finished for the summer. She'd weeded the garden, trimmed the hedge, oiled her bicycle and vacuumed the cottage. Her advance check wasn't due for another two weeks, so she couldn't go shopping. And there were still four hours to pass before she could reasonably go to bed. Then her ears pricked up. Wasn't that someone coming?

Her nerves clenched with terror. What if it were Cal?

She looked out the window. Two cars, Sally's and Dianne's. Not Cal.

Never again Cal. Wasn't that what she'd told him? And he'd listened. Obviously. He hadn't phoned her. Or written. He had enough money to buy a helicopter—a whole fleet of helicopters—and land in her back garden. He hadn't done that, either.

Unlike her, he must have moved on. He was probably already dating someone else, a thought that made her so acutely unhappy she could hardly bear it.

One car door slammed, then the second. Joanna walked

out onto the porch. "Hi, there," she said, rather proud of how normal she sounded. "Why both cars?"

"You'll see," said Dianne. "Do you have any of that scrumptious iced tea you make?"

"I do."

Sally plunked herself down on one of the wicker chairs on the porch. "I'd like some, too. With an extra slice of lemon."

"Is this a deputation?" Joanna asked shrewdly. "Because if it is, you're wasting your time."

"Iced tea," said Dianne. "Move it."

Rolling her eyes, feeling minimally better, Joanna headed for the kitchen. When the three of them were settled on the porch with tea and cookies, Dianne said, "I had a call from my sister this morning. All her latest tests are good, and the prognosis is almost certainly for a full recovery."

"Oh, Dianne," Joanna exclaimed, "that's wonderful news, I'm so happy for her. And for you."

"We were both bawling like babies," Dianne admitted.

"So she's been given a second chance," Joanna said; and heard the words echo in her head.

"Precisely," said Dianne. "Which is why we're here."

Sally chimed in, "Once we've drunk our tea, Dianne's driving me home and you're taking my car and going to Vermont."

"I'm *what?*"

"You're going to see Cal and tell him you'll marry him," Dianne said. "This is *your* second chance."

Sally said, "You can't let a few chunks of rock called the Alps stop you from being happy."

"Because you're not happy."

"The last rose of summer," Sally echoed.

"Not even a rose," Dianne said. "Pickerel weed."

"You're in love with Cal and—"

"How did you know?" Joanna interrupted. "I've never said that to either one of you."

Dianne raised elegantly plucked brows. "It sticks out all over. Just look at you, you're a wreck."

"I'm not!"

"You are," Sally and Dianne chorused.

Joanna, to her horror, put her head in her hands and started to weep. She cried for quite a while, her two friends patting her back and murmuring soothing phrases, then supplying her with tissues to blow her nose. She wailed, "I miss him so! All I want all day is just to see him and touch him and hear his voice."

"Well, of course you do," Dianne said. "You love the guy."

"I just couldn't bear it if he was k-killed. Like Gustave."

"So you're going to be miserable for the rest of your life just because he's a mountaineer?"

"I am miserable," Joanna admitted, rather redundantly given her red nose and tear-streaked cheeks.

"And knowing you," Sally said, "you're in love for life."

"So we've put maps in the car, and a few treats, and it's full of gas. The rest is up to you."

"But," Sally said smugly, "we expect to be invited to the wedding."

Again Joanna's eyes filled with tears. "He doesn't love me! He doesn't believe in love."

"Then it's up to you to make him."

"If anyone can, you can."

Joanna gave one last snuffle. "I don't know about that."

"We do."

"I do know one thing—I've got two good friends," Joanna quavered. "Even if they are nosy and dictatorial."

"That's us," Dianne said. "Now we're going, so that

you can pack and get ready and leave early in the morning.''

"One more thing," Sally interjected. "I dated someone else last week. Twice. In the last four days Albert's arranged for a live-in companion for his mother and he's rented his own apartment.''

Helplessly Joanna began to laugh. "Oh, Sally, that's wonderful.''

"So don't you dare suggest you can't make Cal Freeman sit up and take notice.''

"All right," Joanna said meekly. "I won't.''

Both of her friends hugged Joanna. "Have a fantastic time," Sally added. "I don't need the car for a whole week. But I bet it won't take that long.''

They drove away up the lane, Dianne beeping the horn to the rhythm of the wedding march. Joanna gazed at Sally's neat little blue car sitting in her driveway. She was going to Vermont. Apparently. First thing tomorrow morning.

What if Cal were away? Climbing a mountain? Or staying at a luxury resort with a gorgeous blonde?

She ran in the house and dialed his number. After three rings, Joanna heard his deep baritone say, "Cal Freeman.''

She banged the receiver on the hook. He was there. The rest was up to her.

Maybe the gorgeous blonde was in Vermont with him.

If Cal was with someone else, and she, Joanna, drove all the way to Vermont to see him, she'd be horribly humiliated. Although humiliation was the least of her worries.

I'm going to trust him, she thought, gripping the edge of the table so hard her knuckles were white. He said he had feelings for me. Strong feelings. And he hated it when I compared him to Gustave, who was always changing women.

So I'm not going to.

Cal may not love me. But I matter to him. Somehow.

Holding tight to these thoughts, as though they were talismans, Joanna spent the rest of the evening packing. However, she didn't get to sleep until well past one o'clock, because every nerve in her body was twanging like stretched elastic. In consequence, she overslept the next morning; it was nearly noon before she pulled away from her cottage and drove up the lane in Sally's car.

Tomorrow she'd see Cal again.

She had to trust he'd be glad to see her.

She had to tell him that she loved him.

At five the next evening, Joanna was within one hundred and fifty miles of the little town in Vermont where Cal and Lenny lived. She could have kept going quite easily; but she was tired and hungry, and not at all sure she was up to meeting Cal at nine o'clock at night. So she pulled over at a pleasant country inn that was probably more than she could afford. She needed cosseting, she decided. She could use her credit card; by the time the bill came she'd have her advance from the publishers.

She went for a walk after supper, then to bed. She slept soundly until 5:00 a.m., after which she lay awake listing all the negative outcomes of her unexpected arrival at Cal's house. He was finished with her, child or no child. He'd never love her but would insist on marrying her and then taking off the very next day to Patagonia. He'd be so angry with her that he'd show her the door.

Or else the gorgeous blonde would open the door.

None of these dire thoughts was remotely comforting. At quarter to seven Joanna got up, showered, went downstairs for a breakfast that deserved more than the attention she gave it, then took a short walk around the lake that bordered the inn's formal garden. The sun on the blue water, the pure white water lilies and the quacking of an unseen duck were somewhat comforting. At eight twenty-five she set off.

It was eleven-twenty when she stopped for directions on the outskirts of the town of Madson; at eleven-thirty she turned into Cal's driveway. It was flanked by stone pillars, with a wrought-iron sign that said Riversedge, and proceeded to wind for nearly a quarter of a mile through tall elms and maples, their leaves a cool green roof. Her heart was beating very fast; when she finally drove into the open again, she gave a gasp of mingled pleasure and dismay.

A gracious double-winged Colonial house built of stone, with dazzling white trim and a slate roof set with several charming dormers; expansive stables to one side, garages to the other, boxwood hedges and mature trees shading the front walk. "I have a lot of money," Cal had said to her once. "An astonishing amount of money."

She had the proof right in front of her. How could he possibly believe she wasn't after him for his fortune? A six-figure advance might seem like a great deal of money to her; to him it would be peanuts.

She parked near the garage, and got out. There was no sign of life. Maybe he'd gone away since her phone call; she should have told him she was coming. But how could she? Wasn't she subconsciously hoping that by taking him by surprise, she'd learn his true feelings?

Her heart pounding, she walked steadily toward the handsome door with its mullioned-glass insets. The doorbell was set in highly polished brass; she pushed it firmly.

A breeze wafted the scent of the river to her nostrils; overhead the leaves rustled, as though exchanging secrets. Then the door opened. A manservant swathed in a canvas apron said formally, "May I help you, madam?"

He was neither blond nor gorgeous. In fact, he was as bald as a coot. "I'm looking for Mr. Freeman," Joanna stammered.

"He's out back. Just follow the path 'round the house through the rose garden and go past the paddock. Don't mind the dogs, they won't harm you."

"Is he alone?" Joanna blurted.

The manservant didn't even blink. "To the best of my knowledge, madam."

"Thank you," Joanna gasped, wondering if her mingled relief and terror was as obvious to the man as to her. Cal wasn't in Patagonia. He was here, in Vermont. Alone. Which meant, of course, that in a couple of minutes she'd be face-to-face with him.

Knowing her whole life hung in the balance, Joanna walked around the side of the house. The rose garden was filled with late blooms nodding on their stems, delicately fragrant. On impulse she picked one, a pale cream tea rose whose petals were edged with pink. She'd give it to Cal. One more way of saying she loved him.

Was she really going to tell him that?

A herb garden with an antique sundial supplanted the roses; the gray leaves and purple blossoms of sage brushed her bare ankles. She was wearing her most becoming sundress to give herself courage; it was a clear violet-blue, sprinkled with flowers, hugging her breasts and baring her shoulders, its skirt coming to mid-calf. Now that she was actually here, she wished she'd chosen dungarees and a long-sleeved shirt as baggy as Dieter's pajama jacket. She was quite sure the thumping of her heart must show where the dress lay against her left breast. Cal would probably hear it, she thought desperately, and took a couple of deep breaths.

As she rounded the west wing of the house, she stopped in her tracks. A lazy curve of the river glinted in the sun, caressed by the drooping fingers of willows. Sloping meadows lay between the house and the river, along with a vegetable garden and an orchard of ripening apples and pears;

to her right was a white-fenced paddock. A robin was lustily singing on top of a stone wall espaliered with peach trees.

All this Joanna saw in one quick instant. Because there was more. Near the stone wall was a woodpile. His back to her, shirtless, Cal was splitting logs, the thunk of the ax echoing against the wall.

He was working with a concentrated ferocity that made her heart sink. He did not, to put it mildly, look in the mood for company. Very slowly she walked toward him, her mind totally blank, her feet automatically searching out the uneven flagstone pathway.

Two dogs were curled near the woodpile, sleeping in the sun. One of them raised its head, saw her and gave a short bark; the other woke up and both got to their feet, stretched and headed up the path toward her, their tails wagging.

Mongrels, both of them. Two of Lenny's rescued animals?

As the dogs trotted past him, Cal looked around. He saw her immediately. A shudder ran through his body, his face a mask of shock. The ax continued its downward swing; to her horror Joanna saw it ricochet off the log and strike his hand. Drops of blood sprayed the sinews of the wood.

For a moment the tableau was frozen; she wasn't even sure Cal realized he'd cut himself. Then he looked down, dropped the ax and tried to stem the flow of blood with his other hand. The rose she had picked fell to the ground. Then she was running toward him, her heart racing with a new terror. "Let me see," she said urgently.

"It's nothing."

It was far from nothing: a gash in the ball of his hand at least an inch long. She grabbed his shirt from the woodpile, pressing its clean folds to the wound. "Come on," she said, "we'll have to find a doctor."

"What are you doing here?"

She said frantically, "Later—you've got to have stitches in this, it's too deep just to leave. Hurry up, Cal! My car's around the front, I'll drive you."

She took hold of his elbow and shoved him ahead of her, wondering if she'd ever forget the stark contrast of scarlet and white in the folds of his shirt. Cal, rather to her surprise, obeyed her, striding the length of the pathway past the herbs and the velvet-petaled roses. Joanna ran ahead, opened the passenger door and slammed it shut once he was in. Then she got in the driver's seat, turned on the engine and surged along the green-shadowed driveway.

At the highway, Cal said tersely, "Go left. Joanna, I have to know why you're here."

She pressed her foot to the accelerator, terrified anew by the sodden red cloth wrapped around his hand. "I can't tell you now, truly I can't—I've got to concentrate on my driving. But I promise I'll talk to you later. How far do we have to go?"

"The hospital's the other side of town."

She gave an unconscious groan of despair: the narrow streets of Madson weren't built for speed. Then, as though the word speed had conjured it up, she saw a police cruiser parked in the side road that she had just flashed past. In her rearview mirror, with a strange sense of fatality, she watched it pull out behind her, lights flashing. "Oh, no," she muttered, "I'll have to stop."

She pulled over by the side of the road. The officer got out and sauntered up to the car. "Are you aware of the limit—" he began; then he saw her passenger and the blood-soaked bandage. "Cal!" he exclaimed. "What's up?"

"Ax jumped out and bit me," Cal said with a grin; although he was, Joanna noticed with a distant part of her brain, white about the mouth.

"Okay, let's get you through town quick as we can. You follow me, ma'am."

So the little cavalcade drove very fast through the town of Madson, the siren blaring. Joanna said with a thread of laughter in her voice, "I've always wanted to go through a red light. And with a police escort, no less."

Three minutes later they drew up outside the emergency entrance of a small red brick hospital. The police officer opened Cal's door, saying to Joanna, "Park over there, ma'am, I'll go in with him. And we'll forget about a ticket this time."

Heartened by his wink, Joanna did as she was told. By the time she entered the emergency department, Cal had already disappeared. She sat down hard in the nearest chair and tried very hard to compose herself.

She shouldn't have come. Not once since he'd seen her had Cal smiled at her or indicated in any way that he was pleased to see her. Admittedly, he'd been bleeding rather a lot; but surely that wouldn't deflect a seasoned mountaineer?

The police officer strolled back in and came over to her. "They're stitching him up right now. Shouldn't take too long. You want to go and hold his hand?"

"No, thanks," she said quickly, "I'll wait right here."

"No need to speed on the way home."

"I promise I won't," she said solemnly, and watched a grin split his florid face.

"See you 'round," he said, and left as unhurriedly as he'd arrived.

She rather doubted that he would; she was almost sure she'd be driving back to Nova Scotia in short order. For a moment she had the wild idea that she should simply leave now. Flee and never come back. Why put herself through the pain of rejection?

Cal could always find his own way home.

She pushed herself partway up in the chair. Then she heard Cal's voice down the hall, and the sound of his footsteps. She sank back. Too late. Anyway, hadn't she come here to fight for him? Was she forgetting that already?

She'd never be able to face Sally and Dianne if she simply turned tail and ran.

When Cal reentered the room, his eyes flew to her. His hand was cocooned in an immaculate white bandage. He said harshly, "I wasn't sure you'd still be here."

She stood up, wishing he weren't quite so tall, so formidably self-contained. "I'll drive you home. Do you need to get a prescription or anything?"

"No, they gave me enough painkillers to stun a horse...let's get out of here. I'll never live this down, what with the police escort through town and my own stupidity."

Stupid to react to her presence? Is that what he meant? Joanna turned her back, marched outside and got in Sally's car. By the time Cal was seated, she'd started the engine and was ready to back up. Cal said flatly, "Hold on a minute. I still want to know what you're doing here."

"I'll tell you when we get back to your place and not before. I've been on the road the last two days and I need a cup of strong tea and a comfortable chair."

Briefly he gripped her wrist. "Have you lost the baby? Is that what's wrong?"

Her jaw dropped. "No! Of course not."

"There's no *of course* about it—you miscarried last October."

"I'm taking very good care of myself. Truly, Cal." Joanna shook her arm free, sick at heart that his sole concern should be the baby. "Where's Lenny?"

"Gone for the day."

Fond as she was of Lenny, Joanna was relieved; she didn't need any further complications to a day that already seemed interminable. She'd be long gone from here by the time Lenny got home, she thought miserably, and drove back to Riversedge in a strained silence. Once there, she parked by the garage again and followed Cal through the front door.

Her overwrought nerves took in a brass chandelier, a beautifully proportioned entrance hall and the elegant curve of a spiral staircase. She followed Cal up these stairs, her purse banging against her hip. A bowl of roses against the panes of an oval window, and then the entrance to what must be the east wing of the house. He said briefly, ushering her in, "My living quarters—we'll have privacy here."

She both needed and dreaded such privacy. Not saying a word, Joanna followed him down a long hall decorated with stunning photographs of various mountain peaks, into a living room with a stone fireplace and a bay window that overlooked the river and the faraway, blue-tinted hills.

He said with the same intimidatingly distant courtesy, "I'll make you some tea—I'll be back in a minute."

"I can get it, shouldn't you—"

But he'd already left the room. She wandered over to the window, gazing at a scene whose serenity was utterly alien to her own inner turmoil. She'd say what she had to say and she'd get out.

And this time she'd stay away from Cal. Forever.

CHAPTER FIFTEEN

WITHIN a few minutes Cal was back. "You'll have to carry the tray," he said stiffly.

Joanna went into the well-appointed kitchen, picked up the tray and carried it back into the living room. She poured two cups, passed Cal his, put hers down on a small cherrywood table and said, "I came to tell you the truth."

"And what version of the truth might that be?"

She raised her chin. "You don't have to make this more difficult than it already is."

"I've had the worst few weeks of my entire life," Cal said. "I don't feel conciliatory."

"Then I'm wasting my time."

"For the fourth time, Joanna, tell me why you're here."

She took a deep breath. It was now or never. Her voice high-pitched with nervousness, she said, "I came to tell you I'll marry you. If you still want me to."

"And what brought about this change of heart?"

Go for broke, Joanna. By the looks of it, you've got nothing more to lose. You've lost it already. She lifted her chin still higher. "I love you," she said with a complete absence of emotion.

His eyes narrowed. "You *what?* Since when?"

"I don't know—does it matter? Look, I know I'm doing this all wrong. But I had to come and see if—"

Cal reached out, resting a hand on her wrist, an inner tension in his face gradually relaxing. He said evenly, "For the last thirty-six hours I've been trying to reach you by phone. No answer. Your department at the university would only tell me you were on vacation, and you never told me the names of your friends there. Dead end.''

"Why were you doing that?" Joanna said in a staccato voice.

"My bags are packed and I have a reservation to fly to Halifax at six this evening. To see if I could track you down.''

"What for? You aren't even glad to see me."

"Glad in no way describes how I'm feeling right now."

"Answer the question, Cal. Why were you coming to see me? Because of the baby?''

"No," he said, "not just because of the baby. Because what I've discovered the last few weeks is that I can't live without you. Weeks that felt like a year, by the way."

"You can't live without me," Joanna repeated slowly. It wasn't quite *I love you*. But it certainly wasn't *Here's the door*. She said, "I can't live without you, either. That's why I'm here.''

Although she longed for the reassurance of his embrace, Cal was still keeping a careful distance between them. "So you drove all this way to tell me you love me?" he said in an unreadable voice. "You're brave as a lion, you know that?''

"Not so brave. The next time you go mountain climbing, I won't...but I'm assuming when I say that, that I'll be with you," she babbled. "I'm jumping to conclusions. You haven't said anything about—''

"Finish what you were going to say."

She twisted her fingers in her lap. "The next time you go mountain climbing, I'll be a wreck until you get back. But I can't turn my back on loving you because you might be killed on the mountains, that's what I've come to understand the last few days. The risk of loss is part of love— its dark side.''

"You *are* brave as a lion. One of the many reasons I

was heading to Nova Scotia was to tell you I'm quitting the mountains.''

"You *are?*"

Briefly Cal described his conversation with Ludo, and then what Lenny had said to him about her own fears. "I've always known about luck. That one day, no matter how skilled you are, your luck can just plain run out and that's that. I've had a great innings. But now it's time to move on. It took me a few days to figure all this out...but I finally did.''

"You're sure? You won't resent me and Lenny for that decision?''

"I'm sure." As Cal got up and took a couple of steps toward her, she, too, got to her feet. He rested his hands on her bare shoulders, the bandage soft on her skin, and said with a crooked smile, "Seems to me I've proposed to you several times. Isn't this your turn?''

"You really were coming to look for me?''

"My ticket's on my bureau.''

"Oh." Joanna bit her lip, her heart fluttering like a trapped bird. "I guess it is my turn—to propose, I mean.''

His smile widened; and surely that was tenderness softening the slate-gray of his eyes? "I'm waiting," he said.

Her own smile was both sudden and radiant, withholding nothing. "Cal," she said, "will you marry me?''

"I will, Joanna. As soon as possible, and that's got nothing to do with the baby and everything to do with you.'' Very gently he pushed a shiny strand of hair back from her face. "Don't you see, you make quitting the mountains so easy. Marrying you, living with you, will be the greatest adventure of my life. I know you'll take me places I've never been—you already have.''

Tears filmed her eyes. "You say such beautiful things to me.''

"It's the truth.''

''You don't know what a relief that is, that I won't have to wave goodbye to you not knowing if I'll ever see you again. I would've done it. But I'm so glad I won't have to.''

''But you would have married me anyway.''

''Yes,'' she said simply.

''You really do love me.''

Her happiness was pierced by a sudden pang of loss: Cal didn't—couldn't—love her back. Wasn't pretending to. She said quickly, not wanting to dwell on this, ''My friends Sally and Dianne arrived a couple of nights ago, told me they were sick of seeing me so unhappy and that I'd better hike myself down here and ask you to marry me.'' She batted her lashes at him. ''On bended knee, was more or less the message. But you can do without that, can't you?''

''I have difficulty imagining it,'' he grinned. ''By the way, you haven't asked me the other reasons I was coming to see you.''

''To abduct me on your prancing white stallion?''

''That, too.'' He traced the soft line of her lower lip with one finger, his face full of what was unquestionably tenderness. ''I missed you unrelentingly, day and night. I regretted every word I'd spoken to you in anger, every time I'd pushed you away. I ached to make love with you. But I wasn't in love with you, oh, no. Not me. I'd been in love with Suzanne and it hadn't lasted, you weren't going to catch me doing that again.''

''We were both running scared. Me as much as you.''

''But it took me longer to stop,'' Cal said wryly. Putting his arms around her, as though he couldn't wait for the contact, he went on. ''Yesterday I was carrying a load of logs into the house—I split a lot of wood the past couple of weeks—and thinking about the heat that birch logs throw, when it hit me that because I'd turned my back on love, my heart was as cold as the granite on the Matterhorn.

And that only you could warm it. I stacked the logs on the pile, and I looked around the basement, and for the first time I allowed myself to say that I love you. That I'll love you until the day I die. That somehow you'd found your way to the very center of my being and you weren't going to leave.''

"You love me?" Joanna repeated dazedly.

"I tried to phone you. All day I kept phoning and no answer. I was terrified that you'd moved and that I'd never find you. Or that you'd met someone else. Someone who goes lawn bowling on Sundays. Someone safe.''

"After I first met you, I dated the registrar a couple of times. He was safe and he bored me to tears.'' Joanna stood a little taller in Cal's embrace, wondering if she could trust the evidence of her own ears. "Say it again, Cal.''

"Giving me orders already?''

"You bet.''

He laughed. "I could show you instead.''

"I hope you will. Soon," she said, color washing her cheeks. "But first I want to hear you say it. You know how it is when you've wanted something so badly and then you get it, and yet you don't quite believe that it's real?''

"I'm yours," Cal said hoarsely. "Joanna, I love you. I've probably loved you since the first moment I saw your face in the middle of a prairie blizzard. But it took me this long to admit it, and for that I'm sorry.''

Her voice shaking a little, she said, "You were worth waiting for.''

He undid the clasp at her nape, loosing her hair to flow free on her shoulders. "What are we standing here for when there's a bedroom down the hall?''

"I can't imagine," said Joanna, and started unbuttoning his shirt, her palms seeking the hair-roughened skin of his chest as a flower turns to the sun.

"We've got the rest of the day," he said huskily. "Just

the two of us. Oh, Joanna, I can't believe you're really here. Come to bed with me, then maybe I'll realize this is all true."

"I'm here," she said, "and this time I'm not going to go away. Ever again."

He took her by the hand, leading her down the hall into his bedroom, where they undressed each other, the leaves of the maple outside the window casting dappled shadows on their naked bodies. With slow sensuality, not noticeably impeded by his sore hand, Cal unleashed a storm of desire in Joanna, a desire he more than matched; and inevitably it mounted to its fiery release. Afterward, wrapping her arms around him, her hair coiled in his shoulder, Joanna said, "I feel so close to you, Cal—so unbelievably intimate."

"I love you. So much I don't know how to say it."

"Your body said it for you," she answered softly.

"Darling Joanna. Your hair smells like flowers, yet it's smooth and cool as the river...and I'm the luckiest of men." He hesitated. "There's something I need to say—I want you to know I'm marrying you for yourself. Yes, you're carrying our child, and that's immeasurably precious to me. But it's you I want. You."

"I know that, Cal." She guided his hand to her belly. "I realized I was in real trouble when I found out I was pregnant and I wasn't happy, even though I've wanted a baby for so long. But I wanted you more—I hope you believe me."

"Right after I talked to you on the phone and was so royally turned down, I was sore enough to convince myself that you'd used me for your own ends. That a baby was what you wanted, not me. But it wouldn't wash...I know you too well for that."

"I had you shacked up with a gorgeous blonde," Joanna replied, smiling at him through her lashes. "But then I decided to trust you. And that's when I got in Sally's car and drove here.''

He tweaked her hair. ''Blondes don't interest me in the slightest.'' Then a look of comical dismay crossed his face. ''Do we tell Lenny that you're pregnant?''

''She's a smart kid—she's quite capable of figuring out how long nine months is. In other words, yes.''

''And you're happy to have her as a stepdaughter?''

''Oh, yes. I liked her right from the start. And we share so many interests.''

''She was furious with me when I told her I didn't want her to write to you anymore. Right before she left this morning, knowing I was flying to Nova Scotia, she loaned me her rabbit's foot for good luck.''

''So that's why this has all worked out so beautifully,'' Joanna chuckled. ''I knew there had to be a reason. Do you realize if I'd left a day later, we'd have passed en route?''

''It doesn't bear thinking about,'' Cal said. He kissed her parted lips, his tongue flicking them with lazy sensuality. ''Perhaps I'll ask for the rabbit's foot on permanent loan…and now I think we should get something to eat— you haven't had any lunch. Then we could go back to bed. If you want to?''

She touched him very suggestively. ''Oh, I could be persuaded.''

''Stop that,'' he growled, ''or you'll never get lunch.''

''But I'm eating for two,'' she teased.

For a moment Cal buried his face in her shoulder, holding her so tightly she almost couldn't breathe. ''I'm the happiest man on earth right now.''

Her nostrils were filled with the heat of his skin, her hands were curved around his back, and within her his child was growing. What more could she ask?

Only that Lenny be as happy as they.

* * *

By five that afternoon, Cal and Joanna were up and dressed, and had wandered outdoors, hand in hand, to wait for Lenny. "It's so beautiful here, Cal," Joanna murmured. "I already feel at home."

"I bought the property after Suzanne died. She never wanted to live in the country. But Lenny loves it here, and so do I." He added, "You won't have to stay here all the time—we can always go to New York or London or Appenzell."

Instinctively she knew she could write here. "I can't think of anywhere I'd rather be than here with you and Lenny."

"Talking of Lenny, here she is," Cal said, his fingers tightening around Joanna's.

Lenny had just emerged through the trees, riding a bay Thoroughbred. When she saw her father and Joanna in the garden, she dismounted, looped the reins over the cedar fence and hurried toward them. Then, suddenly shy, she stopped a few feet away. Her jodhpurs had seen better days; her gray eyes were uncertain. "Hi, Joanna," she said. "How did you get here? Dad was going to Nova Scotia to look for you."

"A friend loaned me her car. Your Dad and I were on the same wavelength—we both needed to see each other."

"What happened to your hand, Dad?"

"I saw Joanna standing in the orchard and the ax slipped," Cal said ruefully. "It's nothing, half a dozen stitches. But other than that, your rabbit's foot worked like a charm."

Lenny looked from one to the other; she was obviously bursting with questions that she wasn't sure she should ask. Cal added, putting his arm around Joanna, "Joanna and I are going to get married. We hope you'll be happy for us."

"Oh, yes," said Lenny fervently. "Where will we live?"

Lenny had some of her father's directness, Joanna thought, amused. "How about here?"

"You mean I wouldn't have to go back to school in Switzerland, Dad?"

"We'll all live here, Lenny."

The dawning smile on Lenny's face emboldened Joanna. "I would very much like to be your stepmother, Lenny. I realize that'll take time, big changes can't be made overnight—but I hope you like the idea, too."

With the same fervency, Lenny said, "I've wanted that all along." She gave her father a swift hug, then hugged Joanna, too. "I was afraid you weren't ever going to see each other again. Can I be a bridesmaid?"

"You can," her father teased, "although not in those clothes." Then, with uncharacteristic awkwardness, he added, "There's something else you should know..."

"You already told me you were giving up mountain climbing," Lenny said cheerfully. "Although I haven't figured out what you'll do instead. You're too big to be a jockey."

"Para gliding?" Joanna suggested, giving Cal a sly glance from under her lashes.

"Helicopter skiing," Lenny added.

"I've always wanted to try that," Joanna said thoughtfully.

"Just as long as it's not lawn bowling," Cal said. "But, Lenny, I'm trying to tell you something. About Joanna and me. Something I'm sure you're old enough to understand. Or at least I hope you are. Sometimes when adults—"

"You mean you're pregnant?" Lenny interrupted, looking from one to the other.

Cal looked visibly taken aback that she'd guessed so quickly. "Yes. Yes, we are. That'll be another big change, Lenny. But I hope—"

"I really love you, Dad. But three's better than two and four's totally awesome."

Cal wiped his forehead with a relief that wasn't altogether faked. "Awesome's not a bad word for the way I'm feeling right now."

Joanna put her arm around his waist and smiled at his daughter. "I couldn't agree more."

"Me, too," said Lenny. "What's for dinner?"

The world's bestselling romance series.

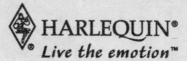

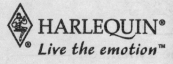

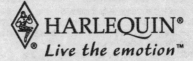

The world's bestselling romance series.

HARLEQUIN®
Presents~
Seduction and Passion Guaranteed!

Back by popular demand...

EXPECTING

*She's sexy,
successful
and
PREGNANT!*

Relax and enjoy our fabulous series about couples whose passion results in pregnancies...sometimes unexpected! Of course, the birth of a baby is always a joyful event, and we can guarantee that our characters will become besotted moms and dads—but what happened in those nine months before?

Share the surprises, emotions, drama and suspense as our parents-to-be come to terms with the prospect of bringing a new life into the world. All will discover that the business of making babies brings with it the most special love of all....

Our next arrival will be
**PREGNANCY OF CONVENIENCE
by Sandra Field**
On sale June, #2329

Pick up a Harlequin Presents® novel and you will enter a world of spine-tingling passion and provocative, tantalizing romance!

Available wherever Harlequin books are sold.

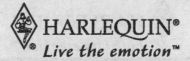

HARLEQUIN®
Live the emotion™

Visit us at www.eHarlequin.com

HPEXPJA

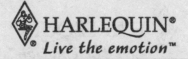